Halfway down the corridor, EJ suddenly stopped. He cocked his head up and jerked to the right. I saw his sudden movement and pulled on the handle to direct his attention back on course.

"C'mon, EJ, this way," I said.

He didn't hear me. He tossed his head, whined, and took off like a bullet down the corridor that we had just started to cross. I had visions of another squirrel chase, but this time I held on tightly to the harness.

"Help!" I called to the others behind me. I couldn't see them anymore, but I heard them chasing my dust.

DARCY'S
DOG DILEMMA

Joni Eareckson Tada

Chariot Books
David C. Cook Publishing Co.

Chariot Books™ is an imprint of David C. Cook
Publishing Co.
David C. Cook Publishing Co., Elgin, Illinois 60120
David C. Cook Publishing Co., Weston, Ontario
Nova Distribution, Ltd., Newton Abbot, England

DARCY'S DOG DILEMMA
© 1994 by Joni Eareckson Tada and Steve Jensen

Scripture quotations are from *The New King James Version*.
© 1979, 1980, 1982, Thomas Nelson, Inc., Publishers.
First Printing, 1994
Cover illustration by Cindy Weber
Cover design by Sandy Flewelling
Printed in the United States of America
98 97 96 95 94   5 4 3 2 1

Library of Congress Cataloging-in-Publication Data
Tada, Joni Eareckson.
      Darcy's dog dilemma/by Joni Eareckson Tada,
Steve Jensen. p. cm. —— (A Joni book for kids)
      Summary: Prayer and reflection help Darcy resolve
the family dispute over acquiring a dog to be her canine
companion.
      ISBN 0-7814-0167-4
      [1. Service dogs—Fiction. 2. Physically handi-
capped—Fiction. 3. Christian life—Fiction.] I. Jensen, Steve.
II. Title. III. Series: Tada, Joni Eareckson. Joni book for kids.
PZ7.T116Dav   1994
[Fic]—dc20   93-36330
                          CIP
                          AC

Read all the books in the Darcy series

JONI EARECKSON TADA founded JAF
Ministries, an outreach that challenges churches
all around the world to fully integrate people with
disabilities. This is one way to encourage *interde-*
pendence—a key word for people with disabilities.
That means people working together to comple-
ment their strengths and weaknesses.

There's another way that interdependence can
happen in the lives of disabled people—with
specially trained dogs! Canine Companions for
Independence (CCI) is a world-renowned
organization which has pioneered the concept of
training specially bred dogs to help people with
disabilities. CCI not only teaches dogs to bring
independence to the lives of the disabled, but
teaches people with disabilities the leadership
skills needed to master a dog.

For more information about CCI, write to:

Canine Companions for Independence
P. O. Box 446
Santa Rosa, CA 95402-0446
or call (800) 767-BARK

To Roy and Phyllis Jensen,
for weaving a love for books into
the family's tapestry of devotion to Jesus
—S.J.

1

"And it's Jessica in the lead rounding the home-stretch, with Darcy closing the distance!" I yelled like a racetrack announcer. "It'll be close, ladies and gentlemen! A photo finish!"

I was flying! Leaning forward to create a jet stream, my wheelchair and I sliced into the cool November air. I stroked the handgrips of my wheelchair to quicken my pace—I had to reach Jessica, who was about to beat me in her power wheelchair. Our racetrack was the long stretch of sidewalk to the courtyard of the mall, with the finish line just inside the lobby of Gibson's department store.

With each second I was gaining ground. My nylon jacket made a swoosh sound as my sleeves slid against the sides of the chair. The tires hummed a low whine over the sidewalk. The evenly spaced concrete tiles added a sense of driving rhythm as my wheels bumped over them—*th, thud . . . th, thud.*

As I reached the mall courtyard, I cut in and out

of benches and potted plants like a downhill skier. The fading shouts of my friends behind me added to the sense of speed and excitement. I whizzed past potted trees, scattering the leaves that lay on the ground. With my chair almost up on one wheel, I careened by an empty water fountain.

I was closing in on Gibson's and my competition, Jessica Crowhurst, an eight-year-old friend who has cerebral palsy. Her mom is my phys. ed. teacher. Jessica and I became close because my friends Mandy, April, and I used to spend our afternoons watching her and teaching her things. But on this November day in front of dozens of startled shoppers, Jessica and I were rivals.

In our cheering section were Mandy and April, my best shopping buddies; our friend Chip; and his friend Mike, whom he had invited so as not to feel outnumbered by us girls.

In order to win, the champion wheeler had to get inside Gibson's department store. I had given Jessica a twenty-second lead from the parking lot. Even though her wheelchair was motorized and had a high-speed setting, I figured her battery pack was no match for my arms and lightweight chair.

I figured wrong. The lobby was fast approaching, and I wasn't gaining ground as quickly as I had anticipated. Some creative thinking was necessary if I were going to win.

As I passed by the last section of benches and trees, I was within thirty feet of Jessica. That's when I saw my chance. The entrance to the department store was made up of a series of doors: two automatic sliding doors situated on either side of a revolving door.

Most people were avoiding the revolving door—shoppers with packages and mothers with baby strollers and children in tow. Because of the crowd of shoppers, a small traffic jam had developed. Jessica stood in line with them, waiting for a chance to squeeze through.

I, on the other hand, gifted with superior intelligence and courage, saw my opportunity to win by going through the revolving door. A big man had just exited, and the door was still spinning strongly. That would give me the chance to slip through without having to stop and push.

I timed my entrance perfectly. A couple of baby strollers still blocked Jessica's path. Within seconds I would be in Gibson's lobby filling my nostrils with the sweet smell of perfume and the sweet smell of victory!

I thought my plan was perfect, but I hadn't counted on how small the distance was between the glass panels of the revolving door. The shrill squeaking of rubber rubbing against glass filled the chamber of the revolving door. The footrests jammed against the curved glass. The revolving door shoved me further against the side, pinning me in front and in back. Panic seized me as I pushed and then pulled on my handgrips.

The wheelchair came to a dead stop. I was stuck.

Too shocked to yell for help, I smiled painfully as Jessica passed through the automatic doors and wheeled herself to the center of the lobby. She parked directly in front of me, her face grinning with victory.

Her grin soon turned into a gasp and then a laugh. "OOOaaah!" she shouted. She seemed delighted with my misery as well as her own triumph.

"It's not funny!" I yelled through the glass. "I'm stuck!"

Finally I convinced her that this was more than one of Darcy's funny pranks. She began wheeling back and forth in the lobby, looking for help.

A small crowd gathered. One man put down his packages and tried to help by pushing the revolving door, but it only jammed me further against the curved wall, and he quickly backed away.

Several clerks came running and tried to coach me out.

"Pull back!" one yelled.

"No!" responded another. "Turn your wheels to the left."

Still another said, "Try rocking back and forth!"

It was no use. I sat quietly, but I was anything but calm. It was getting hot between the glass doors, and I began to sweat. My breathing became rapid.

Lord, please get me out of here, I cried silently.

Mandy and the others had caught up by this time, pushing their way through the crowd. "She's our friend," I heard Mandy say.

"Get me out of here!" I yelled at her when she came up to the glass.

"Cool your jets, Darcy!" she said. "I'm not the

one who got you stuck."

A store clerk joined Mandy. "I called the manager," he said. "She'll bring the maintenance man."

Oh, great, I thought. *I can see it on the evening news: "Girl Arrested for Speeding and Unlawful Entry at Mall!" Or maybe "Girl Starves in Human Goldfish Bowl. Film at 11."*

The crowd of shoppers and bystanders grew larger. I was so embarrassed. I felt my face get hot and flushed.

Mandy sensed my feelings and put her hands up to the glass as if to hold me. She was no longer scolding.

"Don't worry, Darcy, they'll get you out in no time. Safety latches and all that stuff, you know. Hey, just be thankful you didn't get your neck caught in the door. You could have become disabled or something!"

I laughed at her attempt at humor. My accident five years ago had already paralyzed me from the waist down. It was a frightening experience at the time, but I had become used to my wheelchair and my disability. Except when embarrassing things like this happened.

"At least I was unconscious that time," I said out loud, as if Mandy were following my train of thought. "I didn't have friends standing around laughing and a crowd of people gawking as if I were an animal in the zoo!"

Mandy looked around anxiously for the maintenance man. April, Mike, and Chip joined her, forming a shield in front of me.

13

"Another wheeler stuck, eh?" said a voice. "It's usually baby strollers. But wheelchairs? Never had anyone try a stunt like that before. Move aside, kids," the maintenance man said as he approached the door. "Okay, young lady, let's see what we can do here."

He reached up to the center of the revolving doors and pulled a lever. The panels that revolved went limp on their hinges, freeing me up. Then he pulled the door in front of me aside and dislodged my wheelchair. I wheeled out into the lobby to a round of applause.

"There you go, miss. I imagine you won't be doing that again, will you?" He refastened the panels.

"No, sir," I said quietly. I wanted to avoid another one of those school lessons adults love to give.

Chip wouldn't let me. "And?" he prompted.

I felt like a two year old. "Uh, yeah. Thank you," I added with little enthusiasm. I still felt humiliated. Being polite was the last thing on my mind.

The maintenance man and store manager left after making sure I wasn't hurt. The crowd picked up their packages and went on their way, shaking their heads and chuckling. The six of us were left in the lobby.

"So, how about some pizza and soda?" I said to break the tension. "It was hot in there!" I grabbed my throat, gasping and panting.

Everyone could see I was in good humor about

the whole affair, and that gave them the signal to begin chattering all at the same time, giving their version of my adventure.

Jessica remained quiet during the telling of our stories, but as we turned to leave for the pizza parlor, she pulled around in front of my chair and stopped. "I ooowon!" she said.

"Yeah, I know. You won," I answered. "But only because the stupid door wouldn't—"

My lame excuse didn't fly. Jessica sat up on her chair and laughed as loudly as anyone I'd ever heard.

Beaten by an eight year old! Ugh. Embarrassed in front of all those people. Double ugh. What else could go wrong?

"Here's your pepperoni with double cheese, kid."

The man in the white T-shirt that was covered with tomato sauce stains plopped my slice at the edge of the tall counter. "That'll be a buck twenty-five."

"Sorry, but I can't reach the counter," I said. My friends had already gone ahead to find a table, and I had no one to help me. "Could you come around and bring the pizza with you? I've got the money here in my wallet."

He rolled his eyes. He couldn't object too much because I was "one of those" in a wheelchair, but I could tell he was annoyed. We exchanged the money and pizza.

"Thanks," I said.

"Sure. No sweat," he responded with his back to me, already greeting another customer. "Next!"

I placed the pizza on my lap and rolled away. It was exasperating, always having people go out of their way to help me. The frustration showed on my face as I wheeled up to the others.

"What's the matter, Darcy?" Mandy asked with her mouth full. "You're still not thinking of the revolving door scene, are you?"

"No," I said. "I'm just tired of saying thanks, that's all. It feels like my middle name. 'Here's your pizza, miss.' 'Thanks.' 'Got you unstuck from the door, miss.' 'Thanks.' 'Hey young lady, you dropped these keys.' 'Thanks.' Maybe I should just tape a sign to my wheelchair that says, 'In case you help me, push me, reach for me, or save my life—THANK YOU!' "

The group was silent. Chip looked at Mandy and nodded.

"Someone want to pass the Kleenex?" she asked.

That was our signal for telling each other I was having a pity party. My friends did their best to help me break the habit of moaning about my disability. Jessica needed to learn too and so my friends made sure they pointed it out whenever they saw it coming.

"Oh, all right," I huffed and took a big bite of pizza. "Just letting off a little steam."

"So what are we shopping for?" asked Chip, changing the subject.

"Shopping for?" April laughed. "You don't shop for anything, silly. You just shop. You start at one end of the mall and go to the other and see what happens in between."

"Yeah, but didn't you come here to buy something?" Mike asked.

I almost lost my mouthful of Dr. Pepper.

Mandy squealed. "You guys are so dumb. Of course you end up buying something. But that's not why you go to the mall. If that was all there was to it, we'd only be here for five minutes!"

"Okay, guys," April interrupted with an official sounding voice. She wiped her hands on a napkin and stood up. "Lesson number one in mall shopping. Never buy anything the first time through the stores. Number two. Don't stay in any one store longer than fifteen minutes. You'll miss seeing too many people who might be here to see you."

"Whaaat?!" Chip asked, bewildered.

Mike rolled his eyes. "Are you sure you want to do this, Chip?"

I could tell Chip wasn't enthused about the idea of spending the day with a bunch of girls at a mall, but he was too much of a gentleman to say so.

"Yeah, I'm sure. A deal's a deal. We said we'd go if they bought pizza. Here's the pizza and there's the mall. Shop till you drop, right, girls?"

We laughed. "You got it, Chip," I said. "Welcome to our world!"

We dumped our paper plates in a trash can and headed out into the mall, where April continued her lesson.

"This mall is unique, 'cause it's got a hallway between the courtyard and the stores. That means all the stores are on the right side. That makes it simple for covering the territory—you don't have to watch what's on your left. But there are three stories, which confuses things if you're on the third floor and you see kids you know on the first floor."

"So where do you start?" Mike asked.

Mandy answered. "Start on the top floor, of course, and work our way down. The boring stores are all on top, so you get them over with first."

"I knew that," Chip said sarcastically. "C'mon, let's get this over with."

We headed for the nearest elevator, stepped through the open doors, and crowded to the rear. The elevator was made of glass, so we could see the courtyard below. Just as Chip was about to push the button for the third floor, I noticed some people approaching.

"Wait!" I yelled out. "Some people want to get on. Hold the door open."

"Some people" wasn't completely accurate. There were two older girls accompanied by one black dog. "Dog" wasn't entirely accurate either. It looked more like a miniature Black Stallion!

The dog was a Labrador retriever with a large chest and a mammoth head. He led the two girls onto the elevator and parked himself directly in front of me as the elevator door closed. He smiled at me with his tongue hanging out. I felt like I could be his next snack. Only the leather harness around his chest made me feel secure.

"That's a Seeing Eye dog, isn't it?" I said.

"That's right," said the owner. She was tall with

18

short hair and sunglasses. Her friend was the same age and wore a sweatshirt from the University of Delaware. "She would probably like to see the view of the courtyard behind you."

I looked at the owner. "But you're blind. How did you know there's a courtyard behind me?"

"We cheated," kidded her friend. "I told her. She's new in the area, and I'm helping her orient her dog to the mall. After all, no woman in her right mind would let a mall go uninvestigated!"

We all laughed.

"Can I pet him?" Chip asked.

"Her. Her name is Iris," the owner answered. "I wish you could pet her, but she's working right now. I need her to concentrate on her job so she learns every inch of this place. I can't allow cute guys to distract her."

We laughed at Chip, whose cheeks had suddenly grown red. And the real joke didn't hit all of us for a couple of seconds when we realized that the girl had no idea what Chip looked like. It made Chip's embarrassment all the more funny.

The bell dinged, signaling that we were on the third floor. The dog perked up her head at the sound and turned around to face the door.

"Third floor?" the blind girl asked her friend.

Mike responded for her. "Yep. Can't the dog tell you that?"

"Michael!" scolded Mandy.

Mike was being a smart aleck, but the girl didn't seem to mind.

"No, I haven't taught Iris that yet. She's still

learning not to bite off legs that belong to twelve-year-old boys."

Mike instinctively backed away from the dog, and we hooted with laughter. The blind girl and her friend got off the elevator first and turned toward Penney's.

"Hey, how did you know I was twelve?" Mike called out.

"Iris told me. She can smell twelve-year-old boys a mile away," the girl answered. " 'Bye."

We all watched Iris lead the girl around benches and garbage cans to a little boutique where they sold earrings. We headed in the opposite direction.

"Wouldn't it be neat to have a dog like that?" Chip said.

Jessica waved her arms to get my attention, then she pointed to her word board. The board had the letters of the alphabet as well as many common words typed on it. She used the board when she wanted to speak long sentences.

"Maybe," I began sounding out Jessica's words for her. "Maybe . . . if . . . you . . . had . . . one . . . of . . . those . . . dogs . . . pulling . . . you . . . around . . . Darcy . . . you . . . could . . . beat . . . me . . . in . . . a . . . race!" She stopped pointing and smiled up at me.

"Ooh, I'll get you for that one!" I said, pretending to be mad.

"Hey, that's a great idea!" Mandy interrupted. "Not only could the dog pull you around, he'd also keep you from making dumb mistakes like wheeling into revolving doors!"

"Ha, ha," I said, a little miffed at the abuse I was getting. "See if I buy you guys anything for Christmas!"

We made our way around the mall, checking out the sales, the record store, the parrots outside the pet store, and the video game parlor, all according to April's schedule. In between stores, we filled our time talking about how tough prealgebra was becoming, the intramural soccer teams, how boring the announcements were in homeroom, and who liked whom at school. Once in a while my mind wandered. I couldn't shake the thought of a dog like Iris helping me around.

Mandy noticed my absentmindedness. "You've got that look on your face that tells me you're up to something, Darcy. What is it?"

"Oh, nothing," I said. She'd find out soon enough.

2

After our trip to the mall, the school week passed slowly. The anticipation of Thanksgiving made every class feel like a torture chamber. None of us could figure out why teachers even bothered to teach something we were bound to forget anyway. And unlike grade school kids, we didn't waste any time cutting out turkeys or putting on plays about Indians and Pilgrims. It was just work, work, and more work.

What made the week even slower was the intense desire I had to daydream about our trip to the mall and Iris, the dog I had met in the elevator. It was clear to me that the dog provided freedom for her owner. It was as if the girl could actually see what was going on all around her . . . as though the dog really could talk to her and tell her what the scenery was like and whether or not Chip was cute.

"More stuffing, Darcy?"

"Huh?"

"I said, do you want more stuffing?" my mom asked. "Seems you're in another world, young lady. Dreaming of Prince Charming?"

I blushed. My daydreams about Iris had taken so much of my attention that I was even running mental movies during Thanksgiving dinner! I felt more embarrassed because we had so many people for company, including Mandy and her family, Chip and his parents, and Mrs. Crowhurst and Jessica.

I had to answer my mother. I didn't want people to think I was dreaming of anyone special. "No. No. I was just thinking . . . uh . . . how, well, you know, how . . . thankful I am . . . and stuff." It was obvious that I really wasn't thinking about being thankful, but my dad bailed me out.

"You know, Darcy, that's a great idea. Let's tell each other what we're thankful for while we're eating. We guys can talk about football later. After all, before the meal we read the verse that says 'in everything give thanks, for this is the will of God for you in Christ Jesus.' Darcy, you can get us started, since you've been thinking about it the longest. What are you thankful for?"

Oh, great, I thought. *Trapped again.* I scrambled to find something to say. "Well, I'm thankful for . . . my family."

Everybody around the table smiled politely. *Everyone says that,* I thought. *What a nerd. Oh, please, someone say something else!*

Fortunately, there were plenty of people in the room willing to share their ideas. Within a few seconds the words were popping like popcorn.

"Neat friends."

"Health."

"My job."

"Our church."

"School."

"Yuck!"

"That I don't have to do the dishes today!"

"That I have a study hall last period of the day."

"Hold on a minute!" my dad interrupted. "Slow down a bit so everyone can hear. And, Monica, you will help with dishes today. Let's ask Jessica what she's thankful for. All you chatterboxes and motor mouths need to give her a chance!"

Jessica thought for a moment and then spoke in a clear, soft voice. "My word board." She then took her finger and pointed at the letters on the board to begin spelling out more words.

"I . . . can . . . talk . . . to . . . people."

We clapped and cheered. We knew it was more than just a tool for Jessica. It was a way for her to tell people that she was smart and that she had feelings. The word board was special to her mom too, and Mrs. Crowhurst's eyes began to water with tears of joy.

My mom glanced at Mrs. Crowhurst. "Sharing how we're feeling is special, isn't it, Jessica?" Mom asked.

"Honey," she said to my dad. "Why don't we just stop and pray right now? I know you said grace before we started the meal, but maybe everyone could stop and pray silently, thanking God for something special."

"Sure, let's do that." We all stopped chewing on our seconds and thirds of potatoes and stuffing and pushed our plates aside. For a quiet moment, we prayed silently.

There was so much to be thankful for. I was fitting in at school, especially after my fiasco earlier in the semester when I ran for student body president. I was also doing well with journalism club. I had new friends like Jessica and Kendra, an eighth grader who worked with me on the *Jordan Jaguar Journal*. I was able to go horseback riding. No problems on the horizon. Clear sailing. Everything was cool. *Yes, Lord. For all these things, I thank You*, I prayed softly.

Life was good.

And dessert was fantastic! Mom had outdone herself. Only a colossal double-fudge sundae at Baskin Robbins with mounds of whipped cream could have competed with the quarts of ice cream and little dishes of nuts and sprinkles she put out, not to mention hot apple pie and pumpkin custard pie. Dessert time lasted as long as the meal!

While Chip and my little brother, Josh, had extra helpings of pie, Dad and the others told jokes and stories. I just sat back and watched and thought about the people in my life.

My older sister, Monica, with whom lately I wound up in arguments over TV shows or telephone time, seemed more like a human being for change. She was more helpful than usual, getting up to get seconds for me and even cutting up Jessica's food for her.

Josh is a typical little brother. It isn't that I don't like him. It's just that he can do and say the stupidest things sometimes. He drives me crazy. But on this day I had to admit that he seemed like a nice kid. Maybe Jessica was a good influence on him or something.

Dad, as far as dads go, is the best. Still, sometimes he seems like an alien from another planet. The other day Mandy and I caught him bopping around the house, listening to an "oldies but goodies" cassette on my earphones. I was mortified. But again, at times like this, he was so in control, so regular. He made me feel safe down deep inside.

And Mom is Mom. Lately she and I had begun to share more secrets. She answers my strange questions about life without getting nervous and upset. And there are times when it seems she gets really tired with all the work around the house and taking care of ordering supplies and stuff for my disability.

As I was scanning the others at the table, something caught my eye. It was our dog, EJ, playing in the backyard. Dad had shoved him out the back door at the beginning of the meal because he'd gone berzerk when he smelled hot turkey. He'd put his front paws on the lap of Mandy's mom when she was passing the plate and slobbered all over the front of her dress. Mandy's mom didn't like dogs at all, so Dad had no other option.

EJ was a nineteen-month-old golden retriever. His shiny coat and playful prancing in the yard made me laugh silently with pleasure.

As if hearing my thoughts, EJ stopped his prancing and cocked his head in my direction. It was then that I saw them. The same big brown eyes that I had seen in the black Labrador at the mall. His eyes stared at me, telling me something. But what?

EJ was a playmate to me. We took long walks together and slept in the same room. He liked me best, I think, because I was lower to the ground. And I figured we were close to the same age, because one dog year equals seven human years.

It still surprised me, though, when his eyes would catch me like they did. I sat mesmerized while he stared at me.

"Earth to Darcy. Earth to Darcy!" Monica called from across the table.

I loosened EJ's grip on my thoughts and looked over at Monica. It annoyed me that she had interrupted my silent conversation with my dog, but I couldn't explain that to her. I only gave her a whiny, "Wha-at?"

"It's time to clear the table. You got out of helping to set, remember?"

"Yeah, yeah." I sighed and started to wheel around the table, piling plates onto my lap. Mandy and Chip helped me clear, so within a few minutes the table was spotless and the kitchen counter looked like a garbage dump. The kitchen became a madhouse as the sink was filled, plates were scraped, and the dishwasher overloaded. The ladies set about washing the extra pots and pans and stuffing leftovers into plastic containers. Dad offered to help, but Mom sent him off with the other men to watch the bowl games on TV.

"So, what do you want to do?" I asked Chip and Mandy as we pushed the chairs back underneath the table. "Watch football?"

Chip was too good a friend to force Mandy and me to watch. I like sports, but football seems dumb to me.

"Nah, let's do something," he said. "I know, let's go out and play with EJ. He looked lonely during dinner."

"You were watching him?" I asked, as the screen door slammed behind us.

"Sure. Weren't you?"

"Yeah, but . . ." My voice trailed off as we left the kitchen and headed to the backyard. I couldn't imagine that Chip saw EJ the way I saw him. "What did you think of when you watched him?"

"Well, this may sound silly . . . but EJ reminded me of some dogs I saw on TV last night. Service dogs for disabled people," Chip said.

"You mean for blind people, like the dog in the mall?" Mandy asked.

The three of us stood on the deck, and I whistled for EJ. He joined us, wagging his tail and hoping we had brought a few scraps from the table. We didn't have any, so he set off to find a toy to play with.

"No," Chip answered. "These dogs weren't for blind people. They were for people like Darcy, in wheelchairs."

I thought my legs would jump out of the wheelchair on their own. I yelled, "Charles Stanley Dillman!" which is Chip's full name and which he hates, though I think it's nice. "You mean to tell me you found out about these dogs last night, and you waited all this time to tell me?" I was half furious and half excited.

Chip smoothed over my anger and quickly told us what he had seen. "It was awesome, Darcy. I'm sorry I didn't call you, but it was on the late news and I didn't know if you'd be up or not. And then I forgot all about it till dinner. But anyway, you should see what these dogs can do. They pick up keys for people, turn on light switches, even reach elevator buttons!"

I watched EJ pick up a stick in the yard and carry it in our direction. I was too excited to ask questions.

Chip continued, "Volunteers raise puppies. Then when the puppies are fourteen months old, they take them to the training center. The dogs have backpacks. They learn how to pull people in wheel-chairs and do all sorts of stuff. A lot of the dogs looked just like EJ."

EJ reached our circle and dropped his stick in front of me. He lifted his head and looked at me, his large brown eyes speaking again in some lan-guage I finally understood.

"That's it," I said. "Listen, guys, remember when we saw Iris in the mall? I've been thinking ever since about what it would be like to have a dog like that. A dog that is more than a pet. This is so awesome." I stopped and spun my chair around. "EJ is going to be my service dog!" I announced.

Chip and Mandy looked at each other and then

at me. Chip spoke first.

"But, Darcy, EJ isn't a puppy anymore. And it takes a long time to train those dogs. All EJ knows how to do is pick up grungy sticks from the yard and chase squirrels." He wrestled the stick out of EJ's teeth.

EJ barked.

I knew he didn't understand what we were saying, but I was too excited to get technical. "See, he even says he can do it," I said strongly.

Mandy rolled her eyes.

"Get real," Chip said.

"I'm serious. Now I know why we got him in the first place. Just watch," I said. "EJ. Come here."

EJ obeyed my command and stood near my chair, wagging his tail so hard that his backside was going a mile a minute.

"Sit," I commanded. He sat immediately and waited with his ears up.

I continued my demonstration. I had always thought of this as a game, but now I could see that it could actually be useful to me. I took my clip out of my hair and threw it to the opposite end of the deck.

"Go get it, EJ," I said excitedly.

EJ did as he had always done and bolted for the clip. He gently picked it up, pranced around in circles, and eventually made his way back to within three or four feet of us.

"See!" I said to the other two. "EJ can already do that stuff. He'd pass training in no time."

"You mean he'd pass training on how to eat hair

clips!" Chip said with a laugh.

I turned back to look at EJ. He was lying on the deck with the clip between his front feet, slowly pulling each ribbon out.

"EJ, no!" I yelled.

He jumped up with rainbow-colored ribbons hanging from his mouth. He looked really funny, but I didn't laugh.

"Well, he's almost there. He just needs a little more training, that's all."

Mandy was the first to encourage me. "You know, Chip, Darcy may be right. Maybe EJ could do it."

Chip could see he was outnumbered. "Well, maybe there's a lot I don't know. The TV report was only a couple minutes long. Maybe EJ could do it."

That night after our company had gone home, our family gathered around the kitchen table to munch on leftovers. I told them my idea.

"EJ can do it. I know he can. What do you think?" I asked eagerly.

Monica and Josh were hooked the minute I started telling about the dogs. But we all knew it was up to Mom and Dad.

"It's the perfect solution," I continued. "Listen, Dad. How often have you had to pick up a book I dropped on the floor while doing my homework? And, Mom, don't you get tired of pushing my wheelchair when we go on long walks? You say it hurts your back. And watch this—" I dropped my paper napkin on the floor.

EJ, as if understanding the point I was trying to make, picked it up.

"Yes," Dad said. "I see he likes gravy."

EJ was tearing my napkin to shreds.

"That's not the point, Dad. He knows how to get things. After all, he's a retriever. They use these dogs to get ducks and stuff when they go hunting."

Mom and Dad were still unsure, so I pressed my case more strongly.

"Remember the verse from dinner today? 'In everything give thanks.' Everything includes EJ. God gave us EJ for a reason. He's a dog whose talents are yet to be discovered, a dog who will pay his own way, carry his own load, the envy of Rin Tin Tin and Lassie. A dog who—"

"All right, all right," my dad laughed. "I agree a service dog might be a good idea. But we have to investigate this. Who knows, maybe you're not old enough. Or maybe EJ wouldn't qualify. I suspect they start training the dogs at a young age."

"And you need to find out how much it will cost, Darcy," Mom added. "We might not be able to afford it, the training and all."

"Tell you what," my dad decided. "You do all the research. Find out everything, and then we'll talk. Until then, don't get your hopes up. EJ is just a pet, remember?"

I didn't wait for Dad's explanation of how things might or might not work out. I knew EJ was more than just a pet. I was wheeling for the phone.

"Great, Dad! Listen, I'm going to call Chip and

find out where the place is that he talked about. And can we visit there tomorrow? Please? All we ever do on Friday after Thanksgiving is go shopping anyway. You guys can drop me off with Chip and Mandy at the place if it's on the way."

I got more information from Chip and called the TV station right away. Within minutes I had the name and the address of the training center. It was called Canine Companions for Independence and was located about twenty miles away from us.

When I talked to them on the phone afterwards, Mandy and Chip both agreed to come along.

"Chip, thank you so much for telling me about service dogs. And I'm sorry I yelled at you," I said over the phone.

"No problem," he said. "Hey, I'm your friend, remember?"

I hung up the phone and turned to EJ, who stood with me in the hallway.

"Did you hear that, EJ? He's my friend," I said softly. I had always known that. But there was something special about the way he said it, something about his willingness to spend his day off with Mandy and me.

Tomorrow looked like it might be one of the best days of my life.

"Thank You, Lord," I cheered quietly.

I was flying.

3

"We're usually closed to visitors on the day after Thanksgiving," said the tall man with wire-rimmed glasses and a beard. He held his chin in his hand, his eyes narrowed as though to determine whether we were worthy of visiting on such short notice.

The three of us hung our heads slightly, and Mandy and Chip shuffled their feet. We hadn't called ahead. EJ looked up at the tall man with woeful eyes and wagged his tail slowly.

The man kneeled, rubbed EJ's ears, and said, "But since this dog's got just about the prettiest owner I've ever seen, why I suppose we can make an exception." He stood up and smiled. "Now mind you, the dogs are a little upset today. They thought they were going to the store to catch the sale on puppy biscuits. Of course, I told 'em that the way they spent money the last time, I'd be surprised if any of them had any cash left for dog toys. All, that is, except Bruno. He's got a credit card."

34

We finally caught on to the man's humor. Rather than being put off by our visit, he was glad to learn of our interest. And he did like EJ.

"Yep. Good-looking dog you got there. How old? Seventeen, eighteen months?"

"Nineteen," I said, amazed anyone could tell a dog's age.

"Just lucky," he said, reading my mind. "C'mon, guys, I've got rounds to do. None of the office staff is here to give you an official tour, so you'll have to put up with me."

"Thanks for doing this, Mr., uh . . . "

"Hilker," he finished for me. "Dr. Tom Hilker. Dogs around here call me Dr. T. And who are you?"

We introduced ourselves.

"Fine. Now that that's out of the way, let's get moving. Who knows, maybe we'll find a girlfriend for EJ back here." Dr. T led the way from the reception area through wide, swinging doors.

We followed, hearing the sound of dogs in the back. We entered a room full of cages. Each held a dog; there were retrievers like EJ and the black Lab we saw in the mall and other kinds as well.

"What are these dogs for?" I asked, bending down to get a closer look at a couple of smaller dogs. "They look too little to pull someone in a wheelchair."

"Not all the dogs are for people who are paralyzed," Dr. T responded. "Some dogs are used for people who are deaf. This Pembroke Welsh Corgi, for example." He opened the cage of a cute brown and white dog with large pointed ears and short legs. "Bess here is being trained to help deaf people hear things."

"How can a dog do that?" Chip asked.

"They listen for things like doorbells, telephones, alarm clocks. If there is any noise the person should hear, these dogs alert the owner by touching and then point out the source of the sound. They're also taught how to listen for danger.

"And this one," Dr. T said, as we passed by a black and white sheepdog, "will be a social dog."

"You mean a party animal?" I joked.

Dr. T smiled. "Har, har. Did you hear that, Trevor?" he said as he bent down to the dog's level. "She called you a party animal!

"Actually," he said, turning back to us, "social dogs are trained to help people in nursing homes or convalescent centers, places where there's a lot of loneliness. Sometimes social dogs are used for people who are feeling depressed or who are emotionally ill. They may be in hospitals or homes. Dogs love them and help them to feel wanted."

"But don't all dogs do that?" Chip asked.

"Not really. At least not the way that's best," he said as he led the sheepdog out of the pen. "Trevor here, for example, has to be trained not to back away from a person who keeps petting him. Or he may be asked to stay by someone who's angry or crying. He has to be willing to be squeezed real hard by a mentally disabled person who doesn't realize that it hurts. Or he may be touched by a hundred hands during the course of the day at an institution. He can't shy away or get annoyed and snap at them. Not all dogs can handle that.

"But enough about Trevor," Dr. T said, as he led the dog back into the cage. "You want the scoop on those retrievers, I imagine."

We walked to the section of the room where several large retrievers were in pens. Dr. T let two of them out.

"We'll take Buddy and Tanya out for some exercise. Maybe they'd like to play with you, EJ. What do you think?"

EJ barked at the excitement in Dr. T's voice.

It only took a couple of seconds for the dogs to get acquainted. EJ touched noses with one of them while the other one circled. Satisfied that no one was a threat, all three bounded for the door, almost knocking Dr. T over.

"All right, you guys, hold your horses," Dr. T called out as he opened the door onto a large fenced-in yard.

The dogs took off for the other side where there was a ball.

"Normally we'd give them a real hard workout. Today I'll just throw a Frisbee while I talk with you kids." With that he took a Frisbee off a shelf by the window and flung it into the air. EJ spotted it first, took off in a flash, and kept his eye on the saucer the entire time. He beat the others to it, jumped in the air, and snatched it.

"Way to go, EJ!" I called out. "Good catch." The other dogs went after EJ, who was returning to Dr. T for another throw.

"Don't forget to share, EJ," he said, taking the

Frisbee from his mouth. "You'll get these other two jealous before you know it."

While Chip and Mandy took turns throwing the Frisbee, Dr. T explained how Canine Companions for Independence worked.

"The idea behind CCI is to give disabled people as much independence as possible by having the dogs do things that another person would otherwise do. It gives the disabled person more control over her life."

"Chip told me about the TV program he saw," I interrupted. "He said the dogs do all kinds of things like retrieve keys and turn on switches. How do they learn that stuff?"

"Some actions are natural to the dogs. We just teach them when to do it and at the command of the owner. Retrieving something that you drop, for example. That takes advantage of something these dogs like to do anyway, but instead of Frisbees or dead ducks in the water, we replace it with objects like keys or purses or books. I'll show you."

Dr. T called the dogs over by name. EJ followed and sat by my chair, still eager to play but curious about Dr. T's new tone of voice.

"Take your purse there and drop it on the ground, Darcy," Dr. T said. "Buddy," he said to one of the dogs. "Look."

The dog walked over to my purse.

"Get it," continued Dr. T.

Buddy gently placed his mouth around the purse and held it up.

"Bring it here," Dr. T said, pointing to my lap.

Buddy held the purse over my lap.

"Give," said Dr. T, and Buddy let go, dropping the purse in my lap.

I hugged Buddy around his neck as Chip and Mandy applauded.

"Was that hard to teach him?" Mandy asked.

"It takes time, mostly. Some commands are harder to learn. For example, Tanya here is in the process of learning how to pull someone in a wheelchair. The tricky part is to teach the dog to turn left, right, stop, or go. She's not a horse you can lead with a rein. She has to maneuver the wheelchair by herself by simply obeying your voice command."

Dr. T did some more "tricks," as I called them, though they were really more like work. EJ watched quietly. Secretly I hoped he was watching all of this with keen interest. I petted him each time Buddy or Tanya did something. "See," I whispered to him, "you could do that."

Dr. T put Tanya and Buddy back into the kennel when he was done.

"Let me get you some brochures, kids. I'm going to have to get back on schedule pretty soon with the rest of these dogs."

"Sure," I said. "Thanks for taking the time to show us around. Before we go, though, could you tell me how much it costs to get a dog?" I held my breath. Watching all the things these dogs could do, I was dying to have one. But I couldn't imagine being able to pay for all the training.

"Well, that's the neat part of this program," Dr. T answered. "It doesn't cost anything for a disabled person. The dogs are donated, and the cost of training is paid for by donations too."

"But don't you train the dogs for a long time?"

"Sure do. It takes eight months once the volunteers hand them back after puppy training. Each dog has a trainer that spends one-on-one time teaching commands. It's just like school—they even get recess!"

We headed back to the reception area. I still had so many questions. "What kinds of things do they do beside learn to retrieve?"

"Well, we take them to the mall, for example. Two of the dogs stay with a volunteer who watches to be sure the dogs remain where they are told. The other dog leads the trainer through the mall doing the things it learned here.

"We also make the dog experience all kinds of problems like noisy traffic, cats in the yard, loud bangs like balloons popping. Anything that would cause a problem later when they are supposed to be helping their owners."

"Do the dogs ever fail and not become service dogs?"

"Absolutely. About half of them never get paired up with a disabled person. We had one dog, for example, who did great except when it came to loud buses. For some reason it shied back every time it heard a bus. We tried everything to break the dog of that habit. A trainer even slept on the bus with the dog overnight to help the dog feel comfortable. But it never did, and so it couldn't graduate."

We were outside in the parking lot by this time.

"But if the dog does make it, does he get sent to the disabled person?" I asked.

"Oh, no. The future owner has to come here and go through training with the dog. We call it team training—kind of like boot camp, because it's just as hard as the army. You have to study the history of dogs, grooming, nutrition. And then you have to learn how to give commands and get the dog used to your voice and used to you."

"When do the dogs start?" Chip asked.

"They actually start when they're puppies. They join a puppy raising program where they live with a family until they're ready to come here. The family has to teach commands like sit, stay, down, or settle down. They have to learn how to be calm in a lot of different situations. That's the biggest thing. They can't be excited by things or they won't even make it through the eight months here."

My hopes of having EJ be a service dog were beginning to slip. I hated to keep asking questions, because Dr. T seemed anxious to get back to work, but I had to know. "Could EJ be trained?"

"I wondered when you'd ask that," Dr. T said. "He's a little older than most dogs who start here, but there's still a chance."

"But he didn't go through the puppy program," Chip asked. "Doesn't he have to do that first?"

"Not always. If he obeys and if he's calm, then he'd probably do well. Our trainers do the rest."

"You mean EJ could do it?" I asked excitedly.

"It's possible. Are you willing to give him up for eight months while he gets trained?"

"You bet!" My heart raced as I pictured EJ in school and our eventual reunion as my service dog. "What do I have to do?"

"Well, come back tomorrow and I'll go over some of the basic commands you'd have to teach him. I suspect it wouldn't take long for him to learn. You can come back in a week and, if he proves himself, enroll him then. Of course I'll need to talk with your parents about what's involved. They know you're here, right?"

"Yep. I'll probably bring my mom with me tomorrow. Is it okay to come in the morning?"

"Sure. And I'll tell you what. Why don't you surprise your folks with something special? Let me get you a training cape for EJ." Dr. T left us for a moment and then returned with a blue piece of cotton that had the logo of Canine Companions sewn on it. Dr. T hung it over EJ's back and tied the strings under his chest and stomach.

Perhaps EJ sensed that he was somehow destined for greatness. He pulled up closer to me in the wheelchair. I pictured him with a harness, taking me to school, the mall, the stables.

"Well, EJ," Dr. T said as he squatted down next to my dog. "I suspect you are about the biggest puppy ever to join the puppy-raising program!"

When the family saw EJ in his training cape, they really got excited. In fact, they all shifted around their Saturday morning schedules so they could come out to the training center the next day. We got a crash course on what we needed to do with EJ

42

during the next week.

"We don't expect you to bring a Superdog back here next week, Darcy," Dr. T said, "but do your best to get him thinking about the idea." He winked at the thought of my trying to convince EJ about his new role.

I was so excited. I had found someone who really understood dogs!

And I was still flying when we got to church the next morning. It was the first official day of EJ's training, and he had to be exposed to as many situations as possible. If he was going to be my service dog, he had to get used to church!

The ushers in the foyer were a little concerned, but I showed them my letter from the training center and pointed out EJ's blue cape.

"This is a new one on me," said Mr. Briski, the head usher. "We had a Seeing Eye dog once, but pets?"

"He's not a pet, Mr. Briski," I protested. "I know EJ has been our pet, but now he's being trained to work. Just like the letter says."

My dad came up behind me.

"Hi, Jim," Mr. Briski said as he folded the letter and gave it back to me. "Darcy tells me this dog is supposed to come to church now."

"That's right. He needs to get used to being in public places without acting up. Don't worry. He'll be as quiet as a church mouse!"

"Well, okay," Mr. Briski mumbled, missing Dad's attempt at humor. "Right this way."

I sat in the aisle with EJ at my feet and Monica

to my right. I got a lot of stares and plenty of kids petted my dog as they walked by. EJ took it all in stride and only once got up to investigate a Lifesaver that rolled under the pew in front of us. I pulled him back, but he kept drooling and pulling at his leash to get closer to it.

Pastor Rob preached a Thanksgiving message. He said some things I had heard before about thanking God for all that He has given us.

I know that, I thought. *God's been really good to me. The crazy start of this fall is behind me, and from now on it's smooth sailing. Just think. I'll be able to take my dog to school. The other kids will think it's great.*

I pictured their jealous reactions until I realized my pride was getting ahead of me. "Be thankful, Darcy," I whispered to myself as I leaned down and tousled EJ's coat. "EJ is God's gift to you. You didn't earn him."

Just then Pastor Rob said something that made me feel a hot flush. "And be thankful now for the hard times you are going to experience just around the corner. You don't know what they are, but you do know that whatever is in store, the end result will be to make you more like Christ. And that's plenty to be grateful for."

I didn't like the idea of bad news around the corner. But I pushed the thought away. That advice was for those who had nothing special going on at the moment. Not for me. I was about to embark on the best year of school yet. Just me and my dog. What a way to go!

4

"But, Mom!" I protested. "EJ's got to go to school with me. That's part of the training!"

It was Monday morning. I had wheeled into the kitchen with EJ at the end of a leash and that I'll-skip-breakfast-today look on my face. Mom knew in a flash what I was up to.

"Not this week, Darcy. Church was one thing. That was only for the morning, and there weren't six hundred kids distracting him."

"But—"

"And you don't need the distraction either. You're not ready to handle a dog at school all day."

"But, Mom! I told all my friends, who probably told everyone else, that I was going to bring him!"

"You shouldn't have done that, Darcy," Mom said firmly. "Remember, a service dog isn't a pet or a toy. He'll help you make friends, but he's not a tool for you to get attention."

Mom sure had a way of knowing what I was

feeling, but her words still stung. I had to admit I was thinking more of the attention I'd get from taking EJ to class than I was of actually training him. He wasn't ready for the chaos of Jordan Junior High—nor was I sure what I would do the with him the whole day. I had suppressed the thought of his going to the bathroom in the hallway or throwing up on a teacher's shoe. Mom was right. EJ would have to stay home.

It was just as well. Halfway into the morning, I realized that my constant daydreams about EJ were enough distraction. Studying jungle habitat in science class got me to thinking about EJ pulling me through vines and snake-infested brush. Math class was spent picturing EJ at stores handing money over to the clerks and barking when they gave the wrong change. If it hadn't been for the fact that Mr. Dempsey let me work on my article about service dogs for the school newspaper during English, I probably would have daydreamed about EJ learning how to read!

When I wasn't off in space thinking about my dog, I was planning. Every free minute—lunch, study hall, changing classes—was spent planning my days with EJ. Where would be the best place to eat lunch in the cafeteria? What would he do during PE class? Would I bring him into the locker room? I laughed at the thought of a ninety-pound dog running through the showers with someone's clothes or deciding to go for a swim in the pool. No, he wouldn't do that stuff. He's a service dog, I reminded myself.

It wasn't until after school that I could turn my daydreams and plans into action. Chip, Mandy, and I agreed to meet every day after school at my house to put EJ through his paces.

"Okay, let's get organized," Chip announced that afternoon in the family room. Mandy was on the couch, and I was in my chair holding EJ by the leash.

"Who put you in charge?" Mandy asked.

"No, Mandy," I said. "Chip's good at this stuff. Let him do it." I was as fascinated by Chip being in charge as I was happy to have someone take over. I know how to think of crazy ideas, but I need someone else to handle the details.

"Here's the scoop," Chip continued. "We've got to teach EJ five commands by next week. I say we work on one new command a day."

"And then review each one he's learned the following day," Mandy added.

"That's right," said Chip. "Darcy, you've got to be the one to command him. Like this—watch." Chip raised his hand and got EJ's attention. "Sit, EJ!"

EJ sat down, tongue wagging and eager for a reward. I had already taught EJ that command, and he knew what should come next. Unfortunately it wasn't the Canine Companion way to command EJ.

"That was good, Chip," I said, not wanting to discourage him. "But you're not allowed to use hand motions. Only the voice. Here, let me show you."

"Aye, aye, captain," he said, saluting and smiling.

I detected a little bit of hurt, but he was good about it. I turned to EJ, who had stood back up while I was talking to Chip.

"Okay, EJ, sit," I said, without moving my hands.

He cocked his head.

"Sit, EJ, sit," I repeated.

EJ didn't move.

"Push him down on the back end, guys," I said.

"Sit!" I said more forcefully while Mandy and Chip pushed him down.

Whether it was my voice or my friends' pushing, I don't know. He may have sat down out of boredom, for that matter. But whatever his reason, EJ sat, and we had to reward him.

"Mandy, quick! The dog treats!"

Mandy handed me the box, and I gave EJ a biscuit. "Good boy. Good EJ. Okay, guys, let's try it again."

At the end of twenty minutes, EJ had learned to sit just by listening to my voice.

"Look at how many dog treats he ate!" Mandy said, shaking the empty box upside down. "You'll go broke at this rate, Darcy, and your dog is going to get fat!"

EJ was a fast learner, but he got distracted easily and always seemed to do things just a little bit differently. We decided at the end of the training session that it was a success. Sort of.

After school on Tuesday we did our training in the backyard and taught him to stay. He did real well until a leaf blew across the deck and he got up to nose it. Our next attempt was interrupted by EJ getting engrossed in one of the loose strings that hung down from his cape.

Wednesday was "my lap" day. On command, EJ had to learn how to put both paws up on my lap. His first attempt would have been funny if it hadn't been dangerous. I forgot to engage the brakes on my wheelchair, so when EJ plopped his front paws on my lap, the two of us careened backwards towards the stairs of the deck! Chip and Mandy grabbed my wheelchair handles just in time. We decided that EJ would only get a C+ on that command.

Thursday's command required some extra effort.

"Listen, guys," I said to Mandy and Chip. "EJ has been doing all right so far, but this one's going to be hard. He has to learn how to stop at doorways. Dr. T said not to worry if EJ doesn't learn it by the time he goes to the training center, but I think he can do it."

"Why does he have to learn that?" Chip asked.

"Service dogs need to stop at each doorway and wait for the owner's command in case there's something dangerous on the other side," I answered. "Let's go into the garage. There's a wide door that leads out onto the deck from there."

We all headed for the garage, where the three of us and EJ stood in a little circle on the cold concrete floor.

"Now, EJ," I explained in my best Dog English. "You have to stop when we get to the door over there that leads out to the deck." I held his collar as we proceeded toward the door. "This is going to work," I said to Mandy behind me. "Just watch."

Mandy and Chip stayed back and watched. But what EJ and I encountered wasn't what we all expected. Opposite the open doorway on the deck railing was a squirrel. Most squirrels would have run away at the sound of voices or the opening of a door, but this squirrel was either preparing for the Squirrel Olympics or else felt he owned the deck and was under no obligation to leave.

EJ forgot about his future profession as an obedient service dog. He took one look at the squirrel and bolted through the door. I forgot all about EJ's job too and let him go, laughing at the sight of that crazy squirrel as it froze in panic. "Go get 'em, EJ!" I yelled.

We all expected the squirrel to jump off the railing and onto the ground a few feet below. Instead he jumped down onto the deck right under EJ's nose!

EJ skidded to a stop, ducked his head between his front legs, and then did a flip, taking off after the squirrel. The two of them ran in circles on the deck. EJ was not fast enough to make the sharp turns, and the squirrel was too dumb or too stubborn to jump off.

It wasn't until the squirrel saw his chance for escape in my direction that things got hairy. On his third turn around the deck, the squirrel darted toward the opening to the garage. He scooted under my wheelchair as if it were a tunnel. EJ would have tried to squeeze under my chair as well if I hadn't screamed and wheeled backwards out of the way.

"Look out!" I yelled to Mandy and Chip who had by this time retreated into the garage against the wall. "Let the squirrel go through!"

It would have been good advice on my part had the garage door been open. But it wasn't!

Seeing himself trapped inside a room with a monstrous dog and three humans, the squirrel went absolutely nuts. He crashed into every loose object in the garage as EJ followed close behind. Rakes, bikes, cans, and papers flew through the air as the squirrel scratched and scrambled up, down, and over shelves and the dryer and washing machine, knocking over Mom's clean laundry basket. I had never seen such a blur of fur. EJ's barking, the squirrel's frantic chattering, and our screaming made the whole garage look like a scene from a war movie.

The noise brought Monica running in from the kitchen.

"Open the garage door!" I screamed when I saw her.

Monica hit the switch, the garage door motor whined and the chain clattered, sending the squirrel into another orbit. It climbed halfway up the wall, tipping empty clay pots off the shelf and crashing onto the floor.

When the garage door finally opened all the way, the squirrel made his escape, diving from the top of a garbage can onto the driveway and scooting up a nearby tree, flicking his tail in disgust. EJ could only leap a few feet up the trunk, barking angrily.

The chase was over, and the squirrel had won. He left behind him an irritated dog, four stunned people, and a garage that looked like a tornado had hit it.

"So, Darcy," Monica said as we got EJ back into the house, "training EJ to hunt squirrels, are we?" She laughed and I scowled.

"C'mon, sis. Only kidding. There's no way you could have stopped him. That's what the eight months of training will be for, remember?"

"Do you think he'll make it, Darcy?" Josh asked at supper that night. We had only one more day left of training before EJ was due back at the Canine Companion center.

"No problem," I said confidently. On the inside I wasn't so sure. I didn't know what Dr. T would say about the progress we had made in a week. EJ had done okay most of the time but not always. "We'll be fine as long as there are no squirrels!"

"Yeah," Monica complained. "I never knew a squirrel and a dog could do so much damage. The garage looked like your room, Josh, by the time they were through."

"Well, it wasn't my fault the squirrel was there," I said. "Besides, if I had a harness for EJ, I bet I could have held onto him. He'll use one during his training."

Monica looked over at Mom. "How about now?" she asked.

Mom nodded. "Why not?"

Monica left the table but soon returned with her hands behind her back.

"Okay, Darcy, close your eyes," she told me. "And keep them closed until I tell you to open them."

I heard a rustling sound and the jangling of EJ's collar. I could tell he was following Monica into the center of the family room.

"Don't peek," Josh commanded me.

"I'm not peeking," I answered. "Hurry up, Monica."

"Okay, I'm done. You can open your eyes."

I turned my wheelchair to face the family room. My heart jumped and I got goose bumps. Seated like a king in the center of the room was EJ. His blue cape had been replaced by a larger canvas harness with handles.

"Mom and I made it," Monica said. "It's not as nice as the ones they have at the center, but you can hang it in your room as a reminder of EJ while he's away at his eight months of training."

I looked at EJ and then at Monica. Tears came to my eyes. "Thanks, Monica," I said. "You really care about him, don't you?"

"And about you too, kid," she said as she led EJ over to my side. "Now hold on to the handle to see what it feels like."

I made EJ come closer so I could get a good grip on the leather handle. "It feels great, really snug," I said. "How do you like it, EJ?"

EJ licked my other hand.

"See, he's ready to go!" I said. An idea came to mind. "Hey, how about taking him out for a trial run tomorrow? When they train dogs, they take them to the mall where they do tests and stuff. EJ can ride the elevator and pull me around. It will give him a head start on his training, don't you think?"

Monica agreed that it was a great idea. "Yeah, Mom, I'll take them in the station wagon. After all, I did go to all that work to make the harness. It would be a shame not to get to use it once before EJ leaves, don't you think?"

"I don't suppose there are any squirrels at the mall," Dad teased.

"No. No squirrels. Just three thousand crazy teenagers, seven hundred mall walkers, and five food stands with hot dogs and pizza!" Mom replied.

"Tell you what," Dad said. "Why don't we all go? That way your mom and I will be there to help if there's any trouble."

That idea didn't thrill Monica or me, but we agreed.

I pulled EJ's nose close to mine. "Tomorrow we get to show everyone what you're made of!"

After school Friday, we headed out to the mall with great expectations. My parents had decided to make it a big event and invited my assistants, Chip and Mandy.

I was a bit nervous. *Mom's right*, I thought. *It could get crazy with all those kids.*

By the time we got to the mall, it was crowded. There were hardly any places left to park, so Dad dropped everyone off and drove around to find a spot. I got out of the station wagon and stopped for a moment with EJ. I put my hands around the leather grip of his harness and brought his face close to mine.

"Now, EJ, listen. This'll be something new. I'm going to hold on to your harness. You pull. You know, like we practiced after supper in the driveway last night."

He had done a pretty good job. I helped a little by wheeling with my left hand to get him going in the right direction while Monica and Josh called to him from the opposite end of the driveway.

Everyone went on ahead of us. Josh stayed just in front of EJ so the dog would have someone to follow.

"Let's do something simple like go down one side of the mall and then go into a store," I said to the group ahead of me.

"Yeah, like The Limited!" Monica said. "I heard they've got a great sale going on."

"Monica!" I called out. "This is dog training time! We're not here to add to your wardrobe!"

"C'mon, Darcy. This has to be a realistic trip, right? What could be more real than buying clothes for me?"

"I've never been to the mall with you, Monica," said Chip, "but I've seen April shop. If you're like her, I'm not sure which would make a bigger mess—your shopping or the squirrel in the garage!"

Dad caught up with us and stood at the automatic doors as they opened to let us all through.

Our group made a good barrier between the crowds and EJ, so there was a wide open space in front of us. I tugged every once in a while to keep him close to me. Josh made sure he encouraged EJ along the way.

"Pretty good, don't you think, Chip?" I called ahead after a while.

He looked back and smiled with his thumbs up. I smiled back and then stared at the back of his head.

Chip was becoming more special to me. It isn't just his friendship or the fact that he's more mature than the other seventh-grade guys. He makes me feel liked. And I have to admit, he is cute.

I was lost in such thoughts when Mandy turned back to look at me. She had seen Chip put his thumbs up and then watched me stare at the back of his head. She opened her mouth at me and rolled her eyes.

I got embarrassed and gave her a cross look back as if to say, "Don't you dare tell him I was thinking about him."

All of this transpired at our halfway point down the corridor of the mall . . . and that's when things fell apart.

EJ, who had calmly accepted his job to that point, suddenly stopped. He cocked his head up and jerked to the right. I saw his sudden movement and pulled on the handle to direct his attention back on course.

"C'mon, EJ, this way," I said.

He didn't hear me. He tossed his head, whined, and took off like a bullet down the corridor that we had just started to cross. I had visions of another squirrel chase, but this time I held on tightly to the harness.

"Help!" I called to the others behind me. I couldn't see them anymore, but I heard them chasing my dust.

Our detour wouldn't have been so bad, but the crowds were thick and kept EJ from his goal, whatever it was.

"Look out!" I yelled to the crowd in front of me.

Ladies carrying packages on the side watched, frozen in shock. Those unfortunate enough to be in the way had little time to react. The first victim lost his popcorn as EJ brushed by behind his knees and knocked him off balance. A teenager spilled her Coke. An old lady fell backwards into a potted bush. Kids scattered everywhere, laughing and pointing, and moms grabbed their strollers protectively.

EJ was like one of those harness racing horses, and I was the driver being wheeled at breakneck speed, yelling as loud as I could for him to stop and hanging on to his "reins" for dear life.

Dad finally caught up with me. "Let him go!" he yelled.

His strong voice broke through the screams and laughter around me and I obeyed, releasing my grip and coasting to a stop. Free of the weight of me and my wheelchair, EJ continued his race all the faster.

Chip joined us, gasping and wheezing. The three of us stood watching EJ, amazed at his speed and determination. We finally saw him stop at the very last store before the exit.

"What is he after?" Chip wondered aloud.

"I don't know," I answered, wheeling ahead. "But whatever it is, he's going inside the store! EJ, no!"

The three of us started running again, this time with Dad pushing me. When we finally caught up to EJ, we stood for an instant in shock and then began to laugh.

EJ was standing next to a cage full of puppies, licking their noses through the steel wires.

My laughter was soon replaced by disappointment. "Oh, Dad," I said. "EJ will never be a service dog."

"Don't give up so easily, Darcy. Remember, you're not the one who's going to train him. That'll be up to Canine Companions."

"That's right, Darcy," Chip added. "Dr. T will take care of it."

I wheeled up to EJ, encouraged a little by Chip and Dad. "I guess I was hoping EJ would be a Superdog and get to skip his dog classes or something." I grabbed the harness just as the pet shop owner came over holding a big bag of birdseed.

"Sorry, folks. Can't have your friend here hang out too long. My dogs will get jealous. He sure is a pretty one. Gonna be a CCI dog?"

"Yes," I said. "We take him tomorrow. I'm sorry

if he caused any trouble."

"No trouble. Good luck with the dog. Looks like a fine one."

We headed back to the center of the mall where Mandy and the others were waiting. The Red Sea we had parted earlier had sealed back up, and only the popcorn and spilled Coke on the floor gave any hint of our adventure.

After things calmed down and we were sitting around by the hot dog stand, joking and reliving all of EJ's successes from his week of training, I could feel the excitement in me building. I felt especially proud as EJ, during the rest of the visit, obeyed my commands to sit and stay in place in the crowded mall.

"Dr. T is going to be impressed," I told everyone on the way home. "I bet he's never had a better dog enter the program. Right, EJ?"

EJ barked his "yes." In eight months I'd have a service dog!

5

"I'm sorry, Darcy. He can't enter the program," Dr. T said quietly.

My heart sank.

"But he'll learn," I pleaded. "He's never had to stop chasing after things before. And I've only been training him for a week. You told me you're real patient with the dogs. Why not do the same with—"

"It's not that," Dr. T interrupted. "EJ is a fine dog. Squirrels and puppies are distractions we can easily train away. But we can't train away dysplasia."

"What's dysplasia?" I asked Dr. T, angry at whatever this new word meant.

"You remember the X rays we took of EJ this morning?"

"Yeah, but that was routine, right? I mean, EJ is healthy. You've seen him run. He's got bright eyes."

"Oh, he's very healthy. And he's bright. You've done a lot with him. In fact, I'd say he's probably the best dog we've seen who hasn't gone through the puppy program."

His evaluation of EJ confirmed the rightness of my cause. "Then fix this . . . this dysplasia thing!"

"We can't, Darcy. No one can. Dysplasia is a condition of the hips that a dog either has or doesn't have. It's a problem with how the back legs join the hips. Some dogs have joints that fit just fine. Others, like EJ, have a separation."

"But he walks and runs just fine," my mom interrupted. "He doesn't complain at all."

"Well, that's the funny thing about dysplasia. In young dogs it's not a problem. But as they get older, the condition gets worse. It becomes more and more painful and dangerous for them to do things like pull wheelchairs or stand up on their back paws. I'm sorry, but we can't train him. It wouldn't be right."

Dr. T could see my disappointment. In spite of his silly sense of humor, he had always been forthright and gentle with the dogs. Now he turned his gentleness toward me.

"Listen, Darcy," he said as he held my hand. "EJ is an excellent dog. And do you know what's most important about all our dogs here? They love their owners. EJ doesn't need any special training for that. You've already got a companion that loves you!"

That didn't stop the tears from flowing. I had spent a week dreaming and planning and talking about nothing, absolutely nothing but service dogs. I had everyone about bringing EJ to school. Now, through no fault of my own, my dream was over.

All because my stupid dog is . . . is . . . disabled! The thought felt like a hot branding iron, and immediately I felt deeply ashamed . . . but not ashamed enough to stop the flow of more ugly thoughts. *Isn't that the way the ball bounces! Of all the dogs in the world, I have to get one who's a gimp . . . a cripple . . . an invalid.*

No one knew my horrible thoughts. EJ put his head down and walked behind my chair. I was too disappointed to feel sorry for him. Our little group just stood there for a moment until we realized there was nothing more to say.

"Well, thank you for your time," my mom told Dr. T. "Let's go, kids."

We quietly piled back into the station wagon and drove home in glum silence. I spent my time looking out the window, feeling my disappointment rise into anger.

Why does it always turn out like this? Things are going fine, and then they just fall apart. Why didn't Dr. T tell me EJ could have a hip problem? Why did I even bother to try? It's not fair.

My questions left me searching for the real reason for my bitter disappointment. I had already admitted it would be fun to get all that attention, but there had to be more to it. *I want a service dog because I . . . because . . .*

"I want to be independent, Mom!" I burst out of my thoughts and cried aloud. Mom and Monica and Josh were surprised by my outburst. I said it again with conviction, shoving my elbow hard against the car door.

"I want to get around on my own. I don't want to have to ask for help all the time. I want to do stuff myself!" I was angry but didn't feel guilty about it, because I knew my feelings were justified.

The others were silent, watching me as if I was a caged tiger. They knew this wasn't a pity party for Darcy. This was a milestone moment.

I listed my needs for independence. "I've got to be able to do things on my own. I've got to find every imaginable way to do stuff by myself. Mom, you're not always going to be around, or Dad either. How am I ever going to live on my own?"

With each statement I became more and more convinced that a service dog would have been the answer. And then it hit me. A service dog was still the answer!

My anger suddenly evaporated, leaving only a solid conviction. "Mom, I've got it. Think about this! EJ doesn't have to be a service dog after all. He can still be EJ, our family pet, and I can get my own dog!"

It was an entirely new option, and everyone thought about it for a moment.

Then Monica said, "That's a great idea, Darcy. And you wouldn't have to wait for eight months, would you? You could probably apply right away and get in line for a service dog within weeks!"

"And they're free," added Josh.

We all looked at Mom to see what her response might be.

Typical of my mother, she continued to drive without making any comment right away. After a moment's pause, she said what I'd expected to hear.

"Let's talk to your dad about it, okay? It may be a good idea, and it may not be. Don't get your hopes up yet."

I ignored her advice, as did Monica and Josh.

"Another dog! Wow! That's cool!" Josh said.

Monica couldn't believe it. "We'll have golden retrievers in stereo! We'll be the hottest looking family in town!"

While Monica and Josh talked, I went back to my thoughts about a service dog. Moments earlier I was crushed and angry. Now I was planning again. Would I really get another golden retriever? What would his name be? Or maybe it would be a her.

Things will still work out right, I told myself. *This is why God wants you to be thankful. There's always a way to work out a problem. It's His will for me to have a dog, after all.*

Supper time that evening was too quiet for my taste. If there was good news, I was sure Dad would have said something right away. But the subject of another dog didn't come up until after dessert.

"Your mother and I talked before dinner tonight," Dad said as he pushed his chair back from the table.

"And?" I asked.

"And . . . here's the situation. A new service dog is a good idea."

My face lit up. Monica and Josh high-fived.

"But listen, kids," Dad said as he held up his hand. "We can't keep two dogs. We just can't afford the veterinary bills and food bills for two big dogs. If you want a service dog, Darcy, we'll need to find another home for EJ."

The news hit us like a ton of bricks. Monica put down her glass of water. I sat staring at Dad. Josh turned to me and said, "You wouldn't give up EJ, would you?"

My eyes darted around the table. I knew my answer wouldn't be popular, but Dad's option made sense. If I were going to get a service dog—and I was convinced that's what I needed—then we couldn't keep EJ. It was as simple as that.

"Oh, Dad, thanks for taking me seriously about needing a service dog. EJ's great and all, but I know we could find a home for him. Chip, for example. He loves EJ. I'll bet his folks would let him. Right, guys?"

I looked at Monica and Josh for approval.

Monica was leaning her head against her folded hands. She answered, "Yeah, sure," under her breath.

"But EJ's our dog," Josh protested weakly. "You can't. . . ." He stopped, and I thought I saw his eyes watering.

I felt bad, but after all, my being more independent would make it better for everyone.

"Hey, it's what would be best for the whole family," I said with strong conviction. "Having a service dog would be great for everyone. We'd still have a dog, and you guys wouldn't have to help me as much. I like EJ too, but Mom and Dad are right. We can't afford two dogs. And it's not my fault EJ is . . . you know, sick."

The table was silent. Dad looked at everyone. "Monica and Josh, you don't seem too keen on the idea. Are you sure it's okay?"

"Yeah," Monica said shortly.

Josh mumbled, "I guess so." Then, trying to make the best of the situation, he bravely asked, "Will the new dog be like EJ?"

I saw my chance to get Josh on my side. "Sure, Josh. You saw how many goldens they had at CCI. I'm sure it will. And he'll be your pal too, you know. He'll be everyone's dog!"

"Well, okay, then," Dad said. "Let's move ahead with it. We can call Mr. Hilker, I mean Dr. T, tomorrow. We'll have plenty of time before EJ needs to find a home. Do you really think Chip would take him, Darcy?"

I thought of Chip's mom. "Well, maybe, if he asks at the right time. His mom really isn't allergic, and they do have a big backyard. Let me call him." I moved away from the table to go to the phone.

"In a minute, Darcy," Mom said. "We're not going to let this dog discussion get us offtrack. We're having devotions first."

Dad reached for his Bible and read the psalm for the day. My mind wandered with excitement until I heard the words, "I shall give thanks to Thee, for Thou hast answered me."

Yes, Lord! I thought. *You've answered my prayer. Thank You! Thank You!*

Mom and Dad went to a business meeting at church that night, leaving the three of us to clean up after supper. Josh cleared the table and wandered into the family room to play with EJ. Monica and I loaded the dishwasher. We worked silently for a long time.

"So, what do you really think, Monica?" I asked.

She was quiet for a few moments and then exploded.

"What do I really think?!" She slammed a pot into the bin. "Does it really matter what I think or what Josh thinks? If you really want to know what I think, I'll tell you."

She drew in a breath and leaned back against the counter with her arms folded. "All I hear around here is 'Darcy needs this' and 'Darcy needs that.' Why does the entire family revolve around what you need and want?"

I sat in stunned silence. My hands were shaking; I couldn't even put glasses in the upper bin. I didn't want to look at Monica. I didn't want to listen.

"In just ten minutes, you decide we should give up EJ. How do you think I feel? And what about Josh? He loves that dog!"

I finally got enough courage to speak. "Well, you didn't object at the supper table."

"How could we object? Here's poor Miss I-Can't-Walk sitting there, and Mom and Dad trying to help you feel normal. We'd have to be monsters to argue with that. Josh loves that dog more than you do, but he's too afraid to tell his self-centered sister she's hurting his feelings!"

"That's not true!" I blurted. "I do so love EJ. And I don't decide things for the whole family."

"Oh, yeah? Then how come you have the biggest bedroom in the house? How come we only go on vacations where we can get you around in a wheelchair? How come Mom has to have a part-time job to pay for stuff you need? And now, just because you want a big dog to pull you around like a queen on a throne, EJ has to leave!"

I thought fast, trying to find some way to salvage this nightmare of an argument. "Look, Monica, it's better that we get a new dog, anyway, since EJ is sick with this dysplasia thing!"

Monica's eyes widened in furious disbelief. "So that's how you feel? Then why don't we just get rid of you—you're more sick than EJ!" She kicked the rim of my wheelchair, threw the dishrag in the sink, and ran crying out of the kitchen to her room, slamming the door behind her.

I sat alone in the kitchen with the dirty dishes and my thoughts and let the tears pour down my face. I always thought Monica loved me.

I was in my bedroom before Dad and Mom got home from church. I noticed before I quietly clicked shut my door that Monica's door was closed too. I wanted so much to go talk to her, but I still felt confused and guilty.

I lay in bed and blocked out the painful things my sister and I had said to each other. Instead, I built a stronger case for a service dog. By the time I was ready to drop off to sleep, I had convinced myself that I'd done nothing wrong. I did need a dog. Monica would get over it eventually and see that I was right.

6

Monica and I didn't speak to each other at breakfast. Mom noticed it but didn't ask much. Josh took EJ for a long walk through the rain before leaving for school. I pushed away from the kitchen table, leaving a half-eaten bowl of soggy cereal. My fight with Monica had changed the way I saw everything.

I felt restless and anxious all the way to school. My decision to go for a new dog was the right one, I was sure, but no one around me seemed happy. Even Dad and Mom seemed distant, as if they were waiting for something else to happen.

The kids at school had no idea how I felt. Everyone was excited about my article on Canine Companions which came out in the *Jordan Jaguar Journal* before lunch.

"Great story, Darcy," April called to me as Mandy and I waited in line at the cafeteria.

"Thanks." I smiled weakly.

"Yeah," said another girl who was sitting at

April's table near the line. "I didn't know they could train dogs to do things like that. Are you going to get a dog for yourself?"

Several others at the table quieted down to listen to my answer.

"Uh . . . yeah, sure." I didn't sound convincing even to myself, so I said more enthusiastically, "Not until spring though! They only bring the future owners of dogs to the training center twice a year. I'll go to the center for two weeks. That's when I'll meet my new dog."

"Wow! You get off of school just to get a dog?" a boy asked. "Lucky stiff."

The lunch line moved ahead of me, creating a traffic jam behind me as I lingered to talk to the kids at April's table.

"C'mon, DeAngelis. Move your carcass," an eighth grader called out from the back of the line.

"Hey, relax!" April responded, not afraid of anyone. "Deal with it!"

Mandy was behind me and gave my chair a gentle push. "C'mon, let's go," she said. "You can continue your interview later, Miss Celebrity."

I caught up to the line near the silverware bin, but spun around at Mandy as soon as we stopped. "What did you mean by that remark?" I snapped.

"You know . . . the article. The dog you're going to get. Everyone's excited about it." She frowned. "What's the matter, Darcy? You'd think I called you a dork or something. Are you all right?"

"Yes, I'm all right," I said. I was about to tell her everything, including the part about the new dog and my fight with Monica, but decided I'd rather do it alone than in front of the entire planet. "Let's just get our table, okay?" I put my tray on my lap and glanced around the cafeteria. "I'll tell you when we sit down."

Mandy and I found an empty table near the windows. Outside the clouds covered everything except a few patches of blue where the sun shone through. The wind blew dead leaves and litter across the playground.

"That's how I feel, Mandy," I said, nodding toward the scene outside.

"What do you mean?"

"Well, the bright sunshine and blue sky over there are kind of like my getting a service dog in the spring. But how I feel inside is more like the rest of the scenery. Gray, cold, and sad."

"I knew something was going on. You didn't act very excited when the kids asked you about the dog."

"Well . . ." I paused. Sometimes talking out loud about my feelings makes me sound dumb. Then I get mad at myself for how I felt or for what I've done. But Mandy's reassuring smile and eyes told me it would be okay. I could trust her not to be disappointed in me.

I told her everything.

"What hurts most, Mandy, was what Monica said about me. She said I was making all the decisions for the family and that I was self-centered. Seeing her at breakfast this morning was miserable. I don't see us ever speaking again, it was so horrible. What am I supposed to do?"

"I don't know," Mandy said as she began organizing the litter on our trays. "But whatever you do, you'd better settle it before the family retreat. It's only a week and a half away."

We had a four-day weekend coming up, and our church was sponsoring a winter retreat for families at a conference center in the mountains nearby. Half the church was going, it seemed, including Mandy, Chip, and their families. Up until now, I'd thought it sounded like a lot of fun—skiing, snowmobiling, arts and crafts, a speaker, and evening song times around the fireplace in the big lodge.

Now I sank lower in my chair and played with the straw in my empty milk container. The thought of being stuck in a mountain cabin with an angry Monica was too depressing.

"You're right," I said to Mandy. "Something's got to give. And there's something I haven't done that I should do, but I don't know what it is."

"Are you sure you don't, Darcy?"

I felt a little defensive. "Well, I've been trying to be thankful in all things, like Pastor Rob said on Thanksgiving Sunday. But I don't seem to have peace like it says I would in Philippians."

I pulled out a small New Testament from my backpack and found the place I was looking for. "Listen: 'Be anxious for nothing, but in everything, by prayer and supplication, with thanksgiving, let your requests be made known to God and the peace of God which surpasses all understanding will guard your hearts and your minds through Christ Jesus.' "

I closed the Bible, keeping my finger in it to mark my place. "I thanked God for everything," I said in a huff. "For my family, my friends. For EJ. And I thanked Him for a service dog. But I still don't have peace. I feel all confused."

"Maybe you're missing something," Mandy said. "My mom says you need to read all around a verse, so you get the whole picture. What comes before that stuff about praying and giving thanks?"

Reluctantly I opened the Bible again and scanned the page. "Here's the verse before: 'Let your gentleness be known to all . . .' "

"Hah!" Mandy snorted. "Talk about hitting home!"

"Yeah," I said a little sheepishly. "And listen to this verse up further, 'I implore Euodia and I implore Syntyche to be of the same mind in the Lord.' " I didn't have a clue how to pronounce those two women's names, but Mandy and I both got the point.

"Double hah!" I said. "That's Monica and me all right!"

I knew then and there that the whole thing about giving thanks, including my prayers for a service dog, was a side issue. There was something more important than a dog and my independence at stake. What really mattered was sisters getting along with each other.

I looked outside again. The sun had broken through a small patch of sky, but there were angry dark clouds brewing all around it. "What do I do about the storm?"

"You mean, how do you and Monica make up?"

"Yeah. How can I live at peace with someone who won't talk to me?"

"Well, let's see." Mandy thought for a minute. "Do you remember what your dad read at Thanksgiving at your house? I think it was in I Thessalonians."

I had a hard time finding Thessalonians, but with some help from the table of contents I tracked it down. " 'In everything give thanks; for this is the will of God for you in Christ Jesus,' " I read, then I let my eyes scan back a few verses.

"Here it is, Mandy," I said excitedly. " 'Always pursue what is good both for yourselves and for all.' "

The words were clear and full of hope. "Monica was right. I have been self-centered. I wanted the dog more than anything. I was thanking God for what I wanted, but not for what He wanted or what anybody else needed."

I felt relieved to find the answer. But I also felt a little guilty that Josh and Monica were miserable and I wouldn't get to make things right any sooner than supper.

"So what are you going to do?" Mandy asked again.

"Give up on the idea of a service dog," I said plainly. "If that's what keeps me divided from my brother and sister, then that's what I'll give up."

"And give thanks for not being able to have it?"

Mandy's question made me laugh. It sounded strange to be thankful for something you don't have, but I supposed she was right. I guessed that "in everything" sometimes means nothing!

Mandy stood up and picked up our empty trays. I wheeled next to her.

"I really do want to be independent, Mandy."

"Yeah, I know."

"No, really. The dog would have helped me. Having to say thank you every time someone does something for you gets really old."

Mandy didn't say anything as we left our trays at the exit and made our way to the elevator for the next class.

Then she spoke. "Maybe that's the point, Darcy. The problem with being in a wheelchair is not that you can't do things. The problem is that it reminds you that you can't do it all by yourself. But hey, none of us can. That's why we have each other, and why God does what He does. And maybe that's why He wants us to thank Him—to remind us that we can't do it ourselves." She looked me a little nervously, as though she thought I might not like what she'd said.

I smiled at her. "They should declare you the Ann Landers of Jordan Junior High," I teased. "Thanks, Mandy. I hear you."

As we arrived on the main floor I looked out the window by the elevator. The clouds had moved to cover the sun completely. The wind was whipping leaves about, and a few drops of rain had started to fall. It didn't matter. Rain was good. Cloudy days made for cozy afternoons.

I was kind of glad that I didn't run into any of

the family until supper time, when I could face them all at once. Monica was at cheerleading practice after school, and Josh was playing at a friend's house down the street. As everybody sat down at the table, I decided to break the news right away.

"Guys," I said, as I hit my glass with a fork. Everyone stopped reaching for napkins and forks. Monica eyed me, but kept dishing stuff out on her plate.

"I've decided not to get a service dog. Let's keep EJ."

I had secretly hoped everyone would argue with me about my decision, but they didn't.

Josh sprang from his chair and rushed to EJ in the family room. "You get to stay, EJ!" he cried, hugging the dog around the neck.

I looked at Monica and smiled a little.

"Are you sure?" she asked.

"Yeah, I'm sure."

"Darcy, that's a mature thing to do. Are you certain?" Dad asked.

"Yeah, Dad. Hey, if I can't live with a disabled dog, I couldn't live with myself, right?"

The next morning Mom seemed happier, and I even heard Dad whistling in the shower—a sign that everything was A-okay. Josh was like a new man. At breakfast he kept slipping EJ scraps of bacon, and EJ didn't take his eyes off my little brother.

But the same could not be said for Monica and me. We passed the toast and orange juice to each other, but that was it. Our eyes never met. Every breakfast for the remaining week was the same.

Mom would say, "Good morning, girls."

"Hi, Mom," we'd murmur.

We'd sit down. Scarf down toast. Gulp milk. Read the back of a cereal box. Carry plates to the sink. Pick up books. Head out the door. All without exchanging a word.

Finally it was Wednesday, the night before we were to leave for the winter retreat. I sat upright on the edge of my bed. The sky was moonless. A few stars shone brightly and I prayed aloud. "Lord, there's still not peace between Monica and me. I'm not sure what to do about that. But I thank You for my family. And I thank You that I'm not going to be getting a service dog, even though it still hurts." The last words were hard to say. I got a lump in my throat realizing I would never own a service dog as long as EJ lived with us.

Mom and Dad's lamp at the end of the hall reflected into my room and shed its light onto the wastepaper basket by my desk. Sticking out from the basket was the gray folder with the logo of Canine Companions. I had used the information in the folder for my article in the *Journal*. The folder and all its information would be dumped out in the morning with the rest of the week's trash.

With it would go my dream. I fell back into bed and cried softly.

7

The sound of snowplows scraping the street woke me up. The clock on my nightstand read 4:30 a.m.—much too early to get up. I lay back and watched the flakes fall in the light of the street lamp across the street. It was a gently falling snow, lacing the bare branches with an inch of white. It was also the first snow of the season, so it deserved my staying awake to watch.

I became mesmerized by the swirling flakes as they fell. *Good way to get hypnotized and fall asleep*, I thought. I tried to relax under the spell of the streetlight, but staring at it for too long had just the opposite effect. It was as bright as the sun compared with the darkness of the night.

"I've got to do something," I whispered to myself.

To the left of my bed stood my nightstand. On it lay a box of Kleenex, an alarm clock, cream for my dry feet, and my prayer journal that I had started just a few weeks earlier.

Mom had given it to me. "I thought you might like to write your prayer requests and God's answers in it, Darcy," she had said. "And you can write in it the way you write to your Box."

My Box was a big shoe box that I kept in my closet, in the back behind my old stuffed rabbit. It was filled with all kinds of mementos—ticket stubs, pictures of elementary school friends, a couple of old charms from a bracelet that had gone out of style, and very personal letters (written to the Box) about how I felt and what I did.

"Sometimes it's nice to keep your thoughts organized," Mom had added. "You can look back at your journal to see what God has done. And don't forget, it's private. Just between you and God."

I reached for the journal and a pen. I was wide awake by now, so the thoughts came quickly.

Dear Lord,

Life feels like a midnight swim in lime Jell-O. I don't like lime. I'm afraid of the dark. And I'm not getting anywhere. Things aren't going quite right around here. Even though I made the right decision about not having a service dog, nothing makes sense. I feel good about what I did, but I don't know if things are going to change.

My plans and daydreams were a big part of my life, and letting go of them isn't easy. EJ is the only one who stands in my way of having a service dog. I have such bad thoughts toward him. One night I even thought about him dying and how that might get us a new dog, one that wouldn't have dysplasia.

I'm ashamed of myself, Lord, for even thinking that. Josh would call me a murderer. Monica would never speak to me again. Not that that would make any difference. Even though I've made everyone happy, Monica and I still hardly talk. She and I just haven't been close since our fight. Undoing something you've done wrong is simple, but unsaying something is impossible. Her word "selfish" hangs over me like a cloud of smoke. I try to forget, but it's hard. I don't think she can forget, either.

We're going to go on the family retreat today, Lord. Please. Help me see what You want me to see.

Love,
Darcy

I replaced the journal on the nightstand and turned out the light. It was still dark outside, but the snow had slowed down to just a few flakes here and there. I lay my head on the pillow and closed my eyes. Sleep came quickly.

"Wake up, sis. It snowed last night!" Josh pounded on my open door. "You gotta see it!"

I rubbed my eyes and adjusted to the noise of the shower running, the kitchen radio blaring, and doors slamming. Morning had come.

"I know," I mumbled, pulling the covers over my head.

"C'mon, Darcy, get moving!" Josh was tugging

EJ around the house on a leash, and he couldn't contain his excitement. "We're going on the retreat today!"

I lay still, the covers not moving.

"Mom! Darcy won't get up!" he yelled into the kitchen.

"All right, all right," I said as I threw back the covers. "I'm up. Now scram. Leave me alone while I get dressed." I shoved the covers down into a pile at the end of my bed and leaned on my elbows. "And close the door behind you!"

Mom had laid my things neatly on my wheelchair which was angled by my bed within reach. I got dressed quickly and slid into the wheelchair.

"Good morning, Monica," I said with a tired smile as I wheeled into the kitchen. Judging from her response, my prayers wouldn't be answered this morning.

"Hi," she said without looking up from rummaging through her purse. "Mom, have you seen my lipstick? You know, the Maroon Frost I bought last week?"

"Lipstick?!" Josh interrupted his attack on a bowl of cereal. "What do you need lipstick in the mountains for?"

Monica gave him that older sister look. "You'll know why when you get older, Josh. How about it, Mom, have you seen it?"

"Take a look in Darcy's bathroom. I think I saw it on the sink," Mom answered.

Monica flashed her eyes at me. "Did you use my lipstick?"

I tried to smile, but I couldn't. "So what if I did!" I snapped, forgetting my nighttime prayers and anguish. "You're not the only one with lips, you know!"

"Mother!" Monica appealed.

"Monica, go finish getting dressed and stop worrying about Darcy. Darcy, stay out of your sister's things. I've had enough of whatever's been going on between you two. I want you both to start acting like human beings. And do it fast, 'cause we're leaving soon."

Monica huffed out of the room.

"What a beast," I said under my breath.

"Seems you two haven't had much fun the last week or so. Anything you're not telling me?" Mom said.

I sat silently and fiddled with my fork. I didn't want to keep secrets, but it was too hard to explain without making me sound dumb. "No," I said.

"Well, if it's nothing, then let's have a good time at the retreat. Finish your breakfast and I'll fix your hair."

Our family was one of sixty families attending the retreat. We drove for six hours to reach the retreat center, a big place halfway up the mountain. We had left behind three inches of snow on the ground; here it looked like there were three feet of snow! An early snow during Thanksgiving and snow machines made the place seem unreal.

"No December could ever be this white at home," I whispered against the window as we drove by snowplowed mounds and pine trees. There were two ski slopes and a bunny hill for teaching new skiers. Cross-country ski trails crisscrossed the road that led into the center.

We pulled up in front of our cabin, which was one of several built on level ground in the main area by the lodge. It had a stone fireplace in the living room and two bedrooms. All our meals were served in the dining hall, so there was no kitchen. The back bedroom opened out into a screened-in porch. From there you could step into a small yard that was protected by a chain-link fence. We needed that for EJ, because the retreat center didn't allow dogs to run loose. EJ almost hadn't made it on the trip because Monica thought he'd be in the way.

"Like what will he do when we go eat?" she had complained.

The chain-link fence was the perfect answer.

"Besides," I had said, "I'll take care of him. You won't even know he's around." I know I volunteered to take care of EJ because of my guilt over my bad feelings toward him. Maybe if I took care of him, I thought, I'd get over my terrible daydreams about his dying.

Outside our cabin, trails led to all kinds of different places. One trail led from the back to the ski slopes and snowmobile area. Trails in front, paved with asphalt and shoveled clear, led to the lodge, dining hall, and activity center as well as to the frozen pond. Paved trails also led into the woods where a few other cabins were tucked away like Hansel and Gretel chalets.

By the time we unpacked, it was already five o'clock and nearly time for supper. But as soon as the sun came up the next morning, I was raring to go.

"Just one rule, Darcy," Dad said. "You're responsible this whole weekend to make sure the gate is locked on the chain-link fence before you leave the cabin. It's big trouble for everyone if EJ gets out."

"Right, Dad," I assured him.

Dad took Josh up to the bunny hill to teach him how to ski. Mom went to the activity center to set up some crafts and games for the little kids. Monica headed off with some of her friends.

I left the cabin shortly after everyone else to join Mandy, checking on EJ in the yard first. The gate was shut.

"See you later," I called out. EJ barked his complaint.

Most of the kids went skiing. Some, like Mandy and me, rode snowmobiles on the trails. I was able to transfer from my wheelchair onto the snowmobiles without too much trouble. And once on it, I felt the way I did when riding a horse—normal . . . not disabled.

We powered our snowmobiles over trails through fields of snow and beautiful pine trees. The drifts sparkled like diamonds in the sun. The speed of the snowmobiles was the most exciting thing, and the loud noise added to the sense of power. The hour we were given to use the snowmobiles passed quickly.

When our time was up, we returned to the snowmobile shed. "So now what?" Mandy asked.

"Why don't you go skiing or skating?" I answered as she helped me get from the seat of the snowmobile to my wheelchair. "Don't feel like you have to hang around with me all the time."

Mandy was being nice by wanting to stay with me, but I knew she really wanted to ski.

"Are you sure?" she said after she helped me get settled.

"I'm sure. I'm going to the activity center. Mom's there, and Pastor Rob said I could help the little kids make their crafts. After that, I thought I'd spend time writing something for the *Journal*—maybe an article about snowmobiling or something."

"Sounds cool," Mandy said, walking backwards toward her cabin. "I'll catch up with you later, okay?" She waved good-bye and broke into a run.

I headed for the activity center. My trip took me past several families who were making snowmen, throwing snowballs, and goofing off. Further off in the woods I glimpsed three or four older kids sitting on the railing of one of the Hansel and Gretel chalets. Monica was one of them.

She had her back to me, but I could tell she was the center of everyone's attention. Her hands moved rapidly as she described something that was apparently very funny, judging from the laughter of her friends. I was curious and made my way closer.

Monica's voice grew louder. ". . . and then her wheelchair almost bumps into an old lady who goes flying backward into a potted plant. The whole time my sister wouldn't let go. You should have seen it. She just held on like a stupid—"

One of the boys saw me approaching, and his eyes widened. He put his hand up to Monica and then pointed in my direction.

Monica turned, looking very startled, then acted as if she hadn't been gossiping about me. She waved politely. "Oh, hi, Darcy," she said.

"Hi . . ." I answered weakly.

No one else said anything. I sat there, twenty feet from the group, trying to keep my cool. "I, uh . . . I forgot something. I'll . . . see you later." I waved and headed back to the main trail, my face flushing bright red. What an idiot to be so curious—and for thinking the older kids might want to talk with me. And then the way I'd sneaked off—as though I had been the one in the wrong!

The strange acoustics in the woods carried her voice after me even when I was some distance away. "I can't believe it!" I heard her say. "Why didn't you tell me my sister was there?"

I sped away faster so I couldn't hear them anymore. "It was just one of those dumb things sisters do," I said out loud. "Don't worry about it. Monica just wants to impress the boys." The wind stung my cheeks, and two or three tears felt hot against my cold face.

I kept on my course for the activity center. Being with the little kids helped restore my spirits, and seeing Chip come through the door didn't hurt either. The little kids enjoyed going for rides on my lap and reaching things for me. I seemed to be the favorite place for little ones that cried. One little boy even took his morning nap on my lap. For the time being, I forgot about the hurt I felt over Monica.

After lunch we all headed outside to make Disney characters in the snow: Snow White and the Seven Dwarfs, Dumbo, Mickey, and Minnie. We used food coloring to brighten them up. I didn't know my mom was so creative.

Suddenly Chip pointed our attention to the left by the frozen pond. "Uh-oh!" he said. "Look what's coming."

Running along the edge of the pond was Monica. EJ was racing about twenty feet in front of her and pulling away quickly.

"Uh-oh is right," I moaned.

"Darcy, did you shut the gate?" Mom asked, clearly believing that I hadn't.

"Yes, I'm positive. At least I think so." Whenever I get into trouble, I'm never sure if I'm guilty or not.

"Mother!" Monica yelled as EJ caught sight of Mom and me and ran faster toward us. "Get him! He's got Doug's scarf!"

Unfortunately EJ wanted no part of giving up his prize so easily. As soon as he bounded close, he turned left sharply, knocking over one of the seven dwarfs. Chip and my mom took off after him.

"Don't knock over the snow figures!" I yelled, but EJ wasn't listening. He managed to destroy a couple more dwarfs along with Minnie and Dumbo. Mom and Chip knocked over their share too.

Everything was ruined.

"Darcy!" Monica yelled, out of breath as she finally caught up. "Dad told you to lock the gate! How could you be so . . . so . . . "

"Stupid?" I asked with a sneer.

Monica looked at me and knew I was referring to her gossipy comment about me earlier. But she was too mad to be embarrassed.

"Yes, stupid! Do you know what that dog did? I was out walking with Doug, and then along comes EJ—"

"Who's Doug?" Mom interrupted, but Monica ignored her.

"—crashing through with a clothesline full of towels in his mouth. The lady from housekeeping is screaming at the top of her lungs. EJ runs in circles around us, knocking over a garbage can full of smelly junk by the side of the path. I had to use the scarf to get him to drop the clothesline!" Monica's storytelling was extremely dramatic.

"That worked fine, but then I had to chase him all over the place to get the scarf back. And now look at the mess he made!" Monica was furious.

EJ had finished his game of keep away with Chip.

"I got the scarf!" Chip yelled. "Here you go." He handed the scarf to Monica, leaving EJ looking as though we had stolen his bone.

Monica inspected the scarf. "So help me, Darcy, if this scarf is ruined. . . ."

"Who's Doug?" Mom asked again.

Monica couldn't avoid her question this time.

"Oh, just a guy I met. A friend."

"Well, go back and tell your friend Doug that you'll see him some other time. You can stay here and help with the children now—we've got to do something to take their minds off the ruined snow sculptures."

"Aw, Mom," Monica whined.

"I insist. Your sister's been working with these children. You can stop your flirting long enough to get involved a little. Got it?" Mom was angry.

Monica nodded. "I'm going to take the scarf back first," she huffed. Then she walked away, muttering, "Some fun this retreat turned out to be."

Monica's words had stung me again. I had hoped our retreat would be a time to get back together. Now all I could hope for was a weekend where I wouldn't be embarrassed anymore by my dog or my grumpy sister.

EJ walked to the side of my chair, panting softly and looking at me with his deep brown eyes. I wasn't in the mood to think he was cute.

"It's all your fault, you dumb dog," I said under my breath. He hung his head down, ashamed.

"C'mon kids," I heard my mom tell the boys and girls. "Let's go back inside and clean up. Your mothers will be here soon."

I stayed behind and looked at the scene of squashed Disney characters. The colors were puddles in the snow.

"Still feels like lime Jell-O to me, Lord," I said.

8

The supper bell rang out its fifteen-minute warning. I left the scene of destruction behind me and led EJ back to our cabin.

"This time you're staying inside the cabin," I said sternly. "And don't expect me to bring you any leftovers!"

EJ walked close beside me. He knew what an angry voice sounded like, and he wrinkled his ears back and hung his head a little lower than usual. I talked to him on and off the entire way back, scolding him for things he had done as far back as the summer. It wasn't fair of me, but the retreat wasn't going right, and EJ was the only one who couldn't yell back or make fun of me.

I caught up with the rest of the family at the dining table after locking EJ inside the cabin. I knew I couldn't keep him penned up like that all the time, but for tonight I wanted to be certain there would be no escapes.

Supper was the pits. The tomato soup was thin, the cole slaw was watery, the potatoes were pasty, and the grilled cheese sandwiches were greasy. Dessert was just two store-bought cookies. I ate everything, but only after a lot of convincing.

"There's nothing more to eat tonight, so you'd better get filled up," Mom warned.

At least the lousy food gave us something to talk about. There was nothing else to say. Dad was upset with me for not locking the gate. I was upset with EJ for getting me into trouble. Mom was upset with Monica for the time she was spending with Doug. And I was dying to dump more on Monica for back-stabbing me with those ugly things she'd said . . . but I decided not to bring it up. It would have just made things worse. Instead, I listened to Josh jabber on about how much he liked the grilled cheese. He was the only one who was in a good mood.

We went to bed that night without much more conversation. I didn't mind. I was achy and tired from wheeling my chair on the trails that sloped upwards from our cabin to the rest of the retreat grounds. I lay awake for just a few minutes, watching my parents sit quietly by the fire. Their hushed voices, plus the warm glow and the crackling noises of the fire, put me to sleep quickly.

Saturday was supposed to be an "all-out, have-a-blast, laugh-till-you-drop, get-goofy" kind of day. Our youth pastor, Pete, conducted a winter carnival for kids my age. The retreat center let us use the snowmobiles for free all day, so we had snowmobile relay races. An igloo-building contest followed the races. At the end of the contest we tried to pile in as many kids as we could into the winning igloo. It fell apart of, course, and covered everyone with snow.

"Okay, guys!" Pete announced afterwards. "It's free time for the rest of the day. Hot dogs over the fire for supper, and a sleep-over at the DeAngelis cabin tonight. Guys, you get to sleep on the porch, so make sure you bring lots of warm clothes along with your sleeping bags!"

Most of the kids scattered to go skiing. A few, like me, hung around, not so sure what to do. Chip was the first to suggest an activity.

"Wanna go tobogganing, Darcy?" he asked.

"Uh, maybe." I hesitated. I hadn't even considered the idea after watching some kids barrel down the hill the day before. The way they wiped out along the run convinced me I would break a leg if we ever tipped over.

"We'll put you in the middle with plenty of kids in front and back. You'll be plenty safe." Chip seemed to read my mind. "I'll hold on tight. I promise."

Mandy encouraged me too. "C'mon, Darcy. It'll be a blast. I'll sit in front of you. How about it?"

I couldn't refuse my guardian angels. "Oh, all right. You guys will get me killed yet. Next thing you know, you'll have me jumping out of an airplane or rappeling off a cliff!"

I got to the top of the hill riding the snowmobile with Chip. We towed the toboggan behind us while the others trudged up the slope.

"There's Monica!" I shouted over the noise of the snowmobile. I pointed to the ski slope to the right. She was skiing with Doug.

"I wonder what Doug is like," I said to Chip when we had reached the top and were waiting for the others.

We watched Monica and Doug jump a few moguls, criss-crossing each other all the way down the hill.

"I just don't know what's going on, Chip. I feel right about giving up the service dog for the sake of Josh and Monica. And I've forgiven Monica in my heart for the things she said. But things still aren't right. I feel like she's not my sister anymore."

"Have you talked to her about it?"

"No, not really," I answered. "I wouldn't know what to say. I think she hates me."

"Well, why don't you just try reaching out to her? Let her know you still love her somehow."

"But how?"

Chip thought for a moment. "I don't know. You're the one with all the crazy ideas!"

His attempt to make me laugh cheered me just a little.

The rest of the kids caught up with us. We angled the toboggan just right on the edge of the hilltop and then piled on—three kids and Mandy in front of me, Chip and two others behind.

"Hold on tight!" the last kid yelled as he pushed us off.

The roller-coaster drop down the hill was a

scream! The snow sprayed in our faces, and we howled and hollered the whole way. The toboggan scraped and humped over every bump on the hill.

"Whoop! Whoop! Whoop!" we shouted as we slid to a stop at the bottom of the run. Everyone tipped over together and fell out onto the snow, including me. I felt out of control, but Chip held on tight. He made sure my legs stayed above me and that they didn't get caught underneath anyone else. He made me feel safe.

"Awesome!" one boy said as he got up and brushed off the snow. The rest of the group groaned and laughed and threw snowballs.

"Let's do it again!" someone shouted, and everyone agreed. Except me.

"It was a blast, guys, but I think I'll sit this one out." I still felt a little nervous.

Chip seemed disappointed, as if he hadn't made me feel safe.

"It's not you, Chip," I assured him as the rest began scrambling back up the hill. "I just got a little scared when we fell off, that's all. I'd hate to leave here with a broken leg. You guys go on without me. Just carry me over to my wheelchair."

Mandy and Chip looked at each other. I knew what was coming.

"I'll stay with you," Mandy volunteered first.

"Me too," Chip added. He called to the others. "You guys keep going. We're staying here."

I didn't argue. I was all right by myself, but just then I'd had an idea that would require their assistance.

"Thanks for staying behind, you two. Listen. I have an idea."

Before sharing my plan, I filled Mandy in on my conversation with Chip when we were on the top of the hill, adding a few more details about the scene with EJ and the scarf.

"Monica and the others are skiing, right? Well, what if we went to the dining hall and made them some hot chocolate? We'll bring it to the bottom of the ski slope and give it to them when they finish one of their runs. That way Monica will see that I still like her and that I like her friends too. What do you think?"

"Let's try it," Chip said. "Couldn't hurt."

We went to the dining hall where we found the cook glad to help with my plan. He whipped up some hot chocolate on the spot, poured it into big mugs, and put some chocolate chip cookies on the tray—homemade ones this time!

"This'll be great!" I said to Mandy as we left the dining room. Chip had run to get a snowmobile so I could get to the slopes. Mandy carried the tray.

As we approached the bottom of the slopes, I could see Monica and Doug nearing the end of their run. Her bright pink ski suit and dark hair looked striking against the snowy background. I was a little jealous of how pretty she looked. It was no surprise that boys liked her.

I waved and called out. "Hey, Monica!"

She slowed down as she saw me and skied over in our direction. We parked the snowmobile at the edge of the crowd of skiers who were lined up for the lift back up the slope. I recognized a few of them as the group who had been sitting on the railing at the Hansel and Gretel chalet.

"What are you guys up to?" she asked. "Going skiing, Darcy?"

"No. I just thought you and the others would like some hot chocolate and cookies."

Mandy held out the tray a little closer.

"Oh, thanks," Monica said politely, taking a mug.

I watched her face to see if there would be any reaction—like any good feelings toward me. *Maybe she'll apologize right here on the slopes in front of everyone,* I thought. *I'd be embarrassed if she did.*

No need to worry . . . after two sips her face suddenly turned nasty and her eyes, focused on something beyond my head, squinted in anger.

What have I done now? I thought.

The familiar sound of EJ's chain collar provided the answer, and the rest of us turned to see him jogging toward us. He barked and leapt up on Monica, spilling hot chocolate down her front.

"Darcy!" Monica yelled. "How could you be so—"

The lift operator interrupted her. "Is that your dog, miss?" he called.

"Uh, yeah. I mean, it's my family's dog," she said.

"I'm sorry, but you know the rules. Dogs stay on leashes. I've seen that dog loose too often. If you can't keep him tied up, I'm going to have to ask you to stop skiing and stay with your dog back at the cabin. Understood?"

Monica couldn't speak, she was so embarrassed. And angry. Only after the man went back to operating the lift did she continue her lecture at me.

"You were supposed to keep EJ locked up! Now you've gotten me in trouble. Just take that dog back to the cabin and don't come around here again!" She threw the rest of the hot chocolate on the ground and slammed the mug back on Mandy's tray.

"Sorry, Mandy," she added, trying to be polite. "But it's a little hot out here when we're skiing. Maybe later. And, Darcy"—she turned back to me—"you can pay to get this hot chocolate out of my ski suit!" She pushed EJ away with a ski pole and headed for Doug and the others who were waiting in line. We were left standing by ourselves.

I grabbed hold of EJ's collar.

"C'mon, you stupid dog!" I yelled. "I'm tired of you getting me in trouble. I wish you'd never come on this trip!" Inside I thought, *I wish you'd never been born!*

The sleep-over at our cabin that night was a big success. The evening began with roasted hot dogs in the fireplace. It made the place smell spicy and wonderful. We sang a bunch of crazy songs and told dumb jokes.

Then Pastor Pete led devotions. He told some stories that made us laugh, but then he got real serious, real fast.

"Listen, kids. I know we've all got a lot to be

97

thankful for. Most of you don't worry about money or clothes. You get to go on a neat retreat like this. Life's cool, right? But I bet there are some things in life you'd rather not have. For example, think about how you look. Or about your talents. Or your grades. You feel like you'd be great and everything would be fine if only . . . " He stopped and looked around the room as if searching for ideas.

"If only you didn't have something wrong with you . . . like that war zone on the end of your chin!"

We laughed, and a couple of guys made out like they were trying to squeeze a pimple on each other's faces.

"Or that dorky brother who gets into your stuff," Pastor Pete continued. "Or those parents who embarrass you in front of the other kids. All these things are things that you have and can't really do a lot about.

"This is what the apostle Paul says in Philippians 4:11: 'I have learned to be content in whatever state I am.' Look, God didn't blow it when He didn't bless you with great looks or postcard-perfect parents. He didn't mess up when He overloaded your system with extra grease—you know, the kind that makes for more zits. These may be your circumstances, but hey . . . you learn to be content by giving thanks."

"You mean thank God for a zit?" someone jokingly asked.

"Why not?" Pete said. "Thank Him for that zit because it's a sign you're growing up. It'll disappear, eventually. Until then, live with it. It's yours.

And thank God for it. Remember this phrase—'Got it. Thank it.' "

The thought of thanking God for a zit sounded pretty odd, but Pete's words stuck with me as I lay in my sleeping bag in front of the fire. The wood had all but burned up, and only a few glowing coals lay in the fireplace.

Mandy was close beside me, our heads almost touching so we could whisper without being heard.

"What are you thinking about?" she asked.

"Oh, the usual. How things aren't going right even though I'm trying my best to be thankful and loving."

"You mean toward Monica?"

"Yeah. And EJ too. It's usually easy to love a dog, but right now I wish he were dead. And not just because he keeps getting me into trouble with Monica." I confessed my true feelings at last. "If I didn't have EJ, I could probably get another dog. A dog that could be my service dog. But there's nothing I can do about it, and that's what makes me mad. I made a promise to keep him."

"Maybe it's got something to do with what Pete said tonight," Mandy answered. "EJ will live for a long time, and your sister will always be your sister. There's nothing you can do about them except love them."

"You mean they're like two zits on the end of my nose? Hey, do I love those zits. Gotta have 'em—can't live without 'em."

That sent Mandy into a giggling fit.

"Shhh!" I said as I shoved my pillow into her

face. "You'll wake everyone up."

"Darcy, sometimes you are such a nut."

I turned my head and stared ahead at the glowing coals, letting my eyes get hot. "Yeah, I know. A disabled nut with a crippled dog and a socially impaired sister. Thanks a lot."

I said the last phrase with a little too much anger at God. I knew it wasn't right. *I'm sorry, Lord. Please help me.*

Mandy and I remained quiet and listened to the soft snoring around us. The room quickly became cool when the orange glow faded. We hiked our sleeping bags up around us. A gentle wind whistled outside, and I hoped Chip and the guys were warm enough on the porch. Mandy whispered good night and patted my head like we used to do when we were little kids.

I closed my eyes and felt the warmth of Pastor Pete's words, "I have learned to be content in whatever state I am."

"I am learning . . ." I said silently and fell asleep.

9

Sunday morning came up over the mountains bright and sparkling. It was the last day of the retreat. Everyone gathered in the dining hall at eight o'clock for a breakfast of pancakes, eggs, and sausages. The cook had gone all out to make our last meal superspecial. The tables buzzed with excitement as people talked about the weekend.

Halfway through breakfast Pastor Rob went up to the microphone. "Let me have your attention, folks; I'd like to make a few announcements. First, after breakfast you're all encouraged to head back to your cabins and pack. Please be sure the cabins are clean and things in order. Second, be back in time for our Sunday worship service which will begin at ten o'clock right here in the dining room. After that we'll load up and head home."

We all groaned. It was hard to think of leaving the fun and the beauty of the mountains.

"At least Christmas is around the corner," I

whispered to Josh. I knew he hated to leave when he was just getting the hang of skiing the bunny hills.

"But right now we have something special planned," Pastor Rob continued. "I want to present the awards for this weekend's activities."

Monica stood up and leaned over to Mom. "I gotta get back to the cabin. Everything's a mess, and I still haven't done my hair. It'll take me forever to get ready for church."

I didn't believe Monica's story any more than Mom did. We both knew she wanted to spend some time with Doug and didn't care about the awards ceremony. But she had Mom on a technicality. Her stuff was a mess, and her hair did look pretty bad under her scarf. I was surprised she had even come to breakfast.

Mom nodded, not wanting to create a scene in front of so many people. Monica grabbed a sweet roll from the table and took off. Pastor Rob continued his presentation.

"And for the best craft project in the junior grades, the winner is Jimmy Washington!" The crowd applauded and Jimmy got up to get his award. I gave him the thumbs-up as he passed our table.

"I helped him with his craft, Dad," I said. "He was my favorite!" I wished Monica was there to see one of my kids get an award . . . but then, she had no idea what I had been doing in the activity center for two days anyway.

More awards were given out, even one for the

snowmen the children had made with Mom and Chip and me. That should have made me happy, but instead it brought back painful memories of smashed snow, a ruined scarf, and Monica's anger. All I could think of for the rest of the awards ceremony was how far apart Monica and I had grown. There was nothing I could do to make it better.

We used to be close. At least in a year she'll be graduating and going off to college, I told myself. *Then we won't have to bother each other anymore.* I suddenly felt cold and pulled my jacket around my shoulders.

After the awards ceremony, I left the dining hall with my family. Chip caught up with me and asked if he could push my chair.

"Sure," I said. "Have you packed yet?"

"Yeah, I packed when I got up this morning."

"Me too," I said.

"So what do you want to do until church starts?" he asked.

"I don't know. Go for a walk?"

"Sure. I'll walk, you wheel," he said with a smile. "Let's give this place one last good-bye."

I told my mom what we were going to do.

"That's fine, Darcy. But do me a favor—"

"I know," I interrupted. I had heard it a million times this weekend. "Check to be sure EJ is still locked inside the yard! I will, I will."

"I'll run ahead and check it, Darcy," Chip volunteered as we got closer to my cabin. He could tell I had had enough of EJ and the fence. I waited on the trail while Chip shook the gate to make sure it

103

was locked. He turned and gave me the okay sign.

"Sorry, EJ," I called out as the dog whined on the other side. "You're not getting away this time!"

We headed down the path toward the frozen pond and found a sunny spot next to a tall pine tree. From where we stopped we could see a distant snowcapped mountain behind the ski slopes. Chip locked the brakes on my wheelchair and then leaned against the tree trunk.

I felt a delicious warmth inside. Chip had chosen to spend some private time with me. *Maybe . . . maybe he thinks I'm special . . . like, really special.*

"So, how are we doing today?" he asked.

"You sound like a nurse," I said. "We are doing just fine."

"You know what I meant. I just wondered how things are with Monica this morning. I didn't see her around."

"Oh, she's around, all right. Somewhere with Doug probably," I said with a sneer.

"Darcy, that's not her fault."

"What do you mean?" I asked.

"It's not her fault that she met Doug and that she likes him. What would you do if you met someone you thought was really neat? I bet you'd go off and spend a lot of time away from your family too."

"And what makes you think you know what I'd do?" I asked, annoyed that Chip would even think of taking Monica's side.

"I don't know. It just seems like something that happens as we get older. Things change, even in families. You know. We want to spend more time with others instead. Like, do you really enjoy being with Josh?"

"Not really, but I don't treat him like he's dirt."

Chip paused for a few seconds. "Darcy, do you think maybe you're just a little jealous of Monica 'cause she's got a boyfriend?"

I was shocked that Chip used the words "Darcy" and "a boyfriend" in the same sentence, then in the next instant I felt stupid and foolish. He wasn't talking about us, he was comparing me to Monica! I squinted my eyes at him in anger. Leaning forward in my chair, I let him have it.

"Of all the insensitive, dumb . . . I can't believe . . . You don't know anything about . . ."

I was so mad, I couldn't make a complete sentence. Chip, like Mandy, had that annoying habit of asking questions that brought out the truth from me. But I didn't want to tell him I was jealous of my sister.

A voice coming up the trail interrupted our discussion.

"Hi, guys!" It was Monica and Doug walking hand in hand.

"Saying good-bye before you leave this romantic spot, Darcy?" she said with a snicker and a wink at Doug. She leaned over toward him and cupped her hand, saying, "Don't they make a cute couple?"

They both laughed as they walked on.

I could feel hot tears filling my eyes. I didn't know if I was more embarrassed or angry. My nice private time with Chip was ruined before it even got started. And Chip had helped ruin it by comparing me with Monica. But most of all, I felt sick to my stomach that my own sister could be so mean.

I glanced at Chip and saw the hurt and embarrassment on his face too. I didn't know what to do or say. For the first time in all the years I had known him, I was at a loss for words.

"I want to be alone," I finally said, turning my face away from his. "I'm sorry about Monica," I added. Part of me wanted Chip to stay. I wanted to erase the whole icky scene and start over. But he listened to my request and left me.

"See you at the dining hall for church," he said as he shoved his hands in his pockets and walked away.

I watched Chip head back to his cabin. He hung his head a bit and kicked a couple of stones on the trail.

He looks like EJ, I thought. *Why, Lord, is it turning out this way? Everything's falling apart.*

I wheeled away from the pine tree, not wanting to be seen by any more passersby. I headed in the direction of the snowmobile shed, the farthest spot from the rest of the cabins and dining hall. It was the only place I could think of where I was sure I wouldn't run into anybody. I just needed a place to go to cry and get it all out before I had to be back at the dining hall for church service. As I wheeled, I kept my head down, hoping not to bump into anybody else who would see my tears.

As I approached the snowmobile shed I looked up. My aimless trip ended with an idea. At the end of the asphalt trail was a parking area, and beyond that, at the edge of the snow, a row of snowmobiles that hadn't been put away in the shed. They were lined up neatly, probably waiting to be used the following day by the next retreat group. It being Sunday, the equipment manager was not around.

I wheeled up to the edge of the parking lot and looked closely at the nearest snowmobile. The keys were still in it.

Sometimes bad ideas come disguised as good ideas, especially when you're feeling miserable. A ride alone through the quiet mountainside seemed great at the moment.

That's what I need—I thought—*to get away.*

Checking to see if anyone was watching, I wheeled up next to the snowmobile, locked my brakes, and slid off the wheelchair and onto the snowbank. From there I pulled myself on the ground over to the seat of the snowmobile. It was bigger than the ones I had been driving during the weekend, but it was the closest. Besides, I figured they all handled the same way.

I turned the key, and the large engine rumbled like a sleepy monster that had been rudely awakened from its nap. I could tell it was a powerful machine, even though it hummed quietly. My escape would be swift and relatively quiet.

I slowly twisted the handle that controlled the speed, but the snowmobile lurched forward quickly. I almost slid off the seat but had enough sense to hold on tightly to the handlebars and to ease off of the gas. It slowed to a stop, waiting for me to try again. *Maybe this thing really is a horse,* I thought.

Careful to twist the gas handle slowly, I pointed the snowmobile in the direction of the woods and sped away toward a distant grove of pine trees. Excitement built in my heart.

My adventure took me on paths I hadn't traveled before. I ignored the trail signs, keeping the sun directly in front of me and the retreat center to my left. *No point in getting lost,* I thought. Leaving the trails is one thing. Leaving the planet is another!

The scenery might as well have been another planet. The snow, untouched by skis or other snowmobiles, lay like a soft, downy quilt. Tufts of green came up here and there from short pine trees that were buried in the drifts. Mountain breezes sent sprays of snow scattering like diamonds, and the sun dazzled through the branches, sending sharp shadows that crisscrossed in patterns like a spider's web.

Feeling more courage from my success at finding such a wonderful trail, I twisted the gas handle harder. The speedometer read twenty miles per hour. Snow sprayed up around me and in my face as the snowmobile crashed into snow banks like a tank.

The space between trees got narrower after a short time. There was a solid wall of pines to my left, so the only path available was to my right. The opening was between two tall trees. Once I was through, the trail took a sharp right turn which emptied out into a clearing. Suddenly I discovered why the adventure I had taken was not marked as a trail, either for skiers or snowmobilers.

One hundred yards ahead of me was a cliff overlooking the valley below. Its presence was frightening at first. It felt even more dangerous because no adult was around. But when I looked out into the spacious valley and the distant range of mountains, I couldn't resist inching forward.

I slowed down within twenty feet of the edge and turned off the motor. Maybe I was taking chances by traveling so far from the cabins, but I wasn't so dumb as to park right on the edge of a drop-off. Twenty feet away would do just fine, especially when I looked around at the scenery.

Awesome mountains stretched for miles into the horizon. The beauty was so majestic that it made me ache on the inside. I watched the sun and thin clouds draw designs on the valley below. It was absolutely quiet except for the wind in the tops of the trees above me.

"I could stay here forever," I said out loud.

The view was picture-postcard perfect, but the wind had picked up and the cold became more noticeable as a cloud passed overhead. It brought me back to reality.

The others will be looking for me when church starts.

"Let's go, beast," I said to the snowmobile as I started the engine. The sense of danger came back, and I carefully assessed how much room I had to maneuver. Because there wasn't a lot of space ahead of me, I turned the handles to the right before going forward. That was a mistake.

With the front skis turned sharply, I powered the engine to go forward—and the snowmobile tipped over on its side. I was holding on tightly to the han-

109

dles, and when the machine tipped over, my right leg got pinned underneath. I didn't feel any pain because of my paralysis, but I panicked nevertheless.

What if my leg is broken? What if I'm bleeding right now and can't feel it?

My heart beat faster. My head pounded. My blood pressure started to skyrocket.

"Help!" I screamed. "He-e-elp!"

The mountain above me seemed to swallow my calls, spitting them out over the cliff and on into the valley below. It would take a year for my voice to carry down there or even back to the retreat center. Besides, everybody was inside the cabins, busy packing. No one even knew I was gone.

In my confusion I had not turned off the key to the snowmobile, and its engine was still whining loudly. I reached up far enough to turn the key, then lay back, exhausted. The air was fearfully quiet.

I've got to keep yelling, I thought. *It's my only hope.*

I raised myself on my elbow, took a deep breath, and hollered again. "Help! Help! Daddy! He-el-lp!"

I let my screams echo. There was no response.

I collapsed back on the snow in fear and exhaustion. "Lord, help me," I prayed loudly and earnestly. But that was all I could pray. I forgot all about asking Him why things were the way they were. Things with Monica and Chip and my family and EJ seemed faraway and unimportant. This was life-and death-stuff.

I started to whimper. "Please, God. Save me." I closed my eyes and waited.

10

The sky changed quickly. One moment the clouds covered the sun, casting a fearful darkness over everything. The next moment the winds carried the clouds away, letting the sun shine bright in a brilliant blue sky. I soaked in the warmth each time the sun reappeared, relieved for its comfort. I needed the sun for survival. A deep chill had begun to settle in my body as I lay on the cold ground.

"Oh, somebody, please come!" I called again.

Everything's going to be okay, Darcy, a voice inside me seemed to say. *Someone will hear you.*

A warm flush swept over me, and I couldn't tell if it was the peaceful inside voice or if I was beginning to freeze to death. But whatever it was, it relaxed me. And the feeling of peace allowed me to rest and find strength. Every once in a while I called out for help in case there were hikers who had come near the area. Even though no one answered, I wasn't discouraged. It felt strange, but I just knew that calling out was part of my job, whether or not anyone heard me.

I lost track of time. I felt sleepy and almost closed my eyes to take a nap when I heard something in the distance. The sound was familiar, but it wasn't the sound of the woods or the wind or even people.

I laughed. "No. It couldn't be. Not out here! There's no way he could have . . . "

I turned my head in the snow toward the direction of the trail. The sound grew louder . . . it was the unmistakable jangling clink-clink of EJ's collar!

"Here, boy!" I called out. "C'mon, EJ!" I couldn't see him, but I knew he was headed my way. "Over here, EJ!"

My voice grew stronger as I heard the sound of his collar getting closer. Then I saw him. EJ galloped toward me through the snow, his beautiful golden hair shining in the sun. Snow silently exploded around him with each leap he took.

" 'Atta boy!" I said as he finally reached me. He jumped back and forth over my body, licking my face and barking and whining.

"C'mon, EJ, get me out from under this thing!" I instructed him. My words meant nothing. He ran around in circles, yelping now and then as if to play. He didn't seem to realize that I was in real trouble.

"Pull me out, EJ. Pull me." I grabbed his collar, hoping he would get the idea and drag me out from under the snowmobile so I could begin the long haul of dragging myself back to the retreat center.

It didn't work. EJ seemed to think I was trying

to hug him. He just buried his nose in my neck and licked me all the more. This dog was no Lassie or Rin Tin Tin. He wasn't even Benji.

"Go ahead, EJ. Watch me die out here," I said as my hopes began to dim again. "Don't you know you're supposed to go get help?"

Oddly enough, EJ responded to this question as if I had just spoken Golden Retrieverese. He shook loose from my grip and bounded away, back in the direction of the retreat center.

"Tell them I'm stuck, EJ!" I called out.

This wasn't TV. EJ didn't speak English. And no one would think of following a dog who was well known for escaping from his pen. He wasn't a trained dog anyone would trust. He was just EJ.

In spite of all this, I held on to the hope that somehow he would bring help.

I knew it would take quite a while for help to come, and I spent the time watching the clouds go by. I soon became anxious again. I checked the snow to see if there was any blood coming from my leg and reassured myself that at least I wasn't bleeding to death. I still called out for help every once in a while, just in case hikers or cross-country skiers happened by.

I looked at my watch. Only three minutes had gone by since EJ left. I grew more anxious. I must be crazy for thinking EJ would actually bring somebody back. He's just a dumb animal!

"Okay, Lord," I said. "I guess it's serious talking time now." I began by singing a song my mom used to sing to me when I was in the hospital.

Safe am I, safe am I
In the hollow of His hand.
Sheltered o'er, sheltered o'er,
In His love forever more.
No ill can harm me,
No foe alarm me,
For He keeps both day and night.
Safe am I, safe am I
In the hollow of His hand.

God used the song in a special way, because I gradually felt safe and secure inside. The kind of safety that I felt when I was in the hospital, looking at all those tubes and blinking machines attached to me. It was a safety that I had not known in a long time. As the voice inside me had told me someone would come, it now told me I would be all right. God would take care of me.

Pete's Bible verse from the night before came to mind again. *For I have learned to be content in whatever state I am.*

"Yes, Lord," I prayed. "I have learned. This feeling of safety is from You, and that makes me content. I don't like being here in this stupid predicament, but I know You're here with me. Thank You."

I continued talking to God until I was suddenly interrupted.

"Da-a-ar-ceey!" a voice called out slow and clear.

I was so surprised to hear another voice that it took me a few seconds to find my own.

"Over here! I'm over here!"

The jangling of EJ's collar accompanied the next

call of my rescuer—Monica!

"Darcy, I'm coming!" she yelled. "Hold on! Don't let go!"

Don't let go? I laughed. Monica must have thought I was hanging over the edge of the cliff.

"Don't worry!" I screamed back. "I'm not going anywhere!"

I could hear EJ barking excitedly, and then I saw them running through the snow together, EJ stopping every once in a while to let Monica catch up.

"Darcy!" she cried with a smile as soon as she saw me. She fell to her knees by my side and hugged me tightly. "Oh, Darcy, are you all right?"

"Not quite," I said, with very little emotion. I had gotten used to my situation. "I'm stuck. Get me out, will you?"

Monica got up and tried to tip the snowmobile back. The machine was too heavy and she slipped in the snow, unable to get a firm footing.

"I know," she said. "I'll dig under and around your leg. It'll create a space for you to slide out."

"Not bad, Sis," I laughed. "You get an A+ in lifesaving. Maybe Doug's been a good influence, after all."

She blushed at my remark and got busy. EJ caught on to the idea and began digging too.

There I was, flat on my back, pinned under a snowmobile, and who should my rescuers be but the very ones about whom I had been complaining for the last few weeks.

"Dad always said You had a sense of humor, Lord," I prayed silently.

Monica made good progress. I tried to help by tugging at my paralyzed legs every once in a while.

"Where's everyone else?" I asked as Monica and EJ kept digging. "How come you're the only ones who came?"

"Mom sent me to look for you when you didn't show up for church. Chip didn't know where you were, and neither did Mandy. We figured you were out for a wheel by yourself because of what had happened with Chip. I told Mom and Dad I probably had something to do with you going off somewhere too," she said with a hint of guilt. "Dad said I should go find you."

"But how did you know to come here?"

"It was EJ. He found me looking for you and started barking and jumping up and down as if something was wrong. I figured he must know what was up, because I had looked everywhere on the grounds of the retreat center."

She stopped for a moment to catch her breath. The snowmobile sat like a bridge over the tunnel Monica and EJ had made.

"Almost to your foot, I think," she said as she reached way under to pull out more snow.

"Try it now." She dusted off her gloves and came around to my back. I dragged my body back over the snow while Monica pulled me by the shoulders. Gradually my leg was visible again. EJ leapt back and forth over my legs, as if he'd just dug up a bone from the yard.

"Ta-da!" Monica shouted. "We did it! C'mon, kid. Let's get you back before you freeze. Look at you. Your lips are almost blue."

With my leg pinned under the snowmobile, my blood had not circulated well. The breeze had picked up, and the cold snow didn't help matters.

"Here. Let me put my coat over you."

"How are we going to get back?" I asked. "I can't drag myself there. I'm too weak."

"No problem. I'll carry you," Monica said. "Cheerleading isn't a completely wasted activity, you know. I've carried bigger girls than you on my shoulders. Here, I'll get down on the ground next to you. You roll on top like you're going to go for a piggyback ride."

We made several attempts before Monica could stand up with me on her back. I was a deadweight, hanging by my arms around her neck. I couldn't help her at all. She'd almost have me, then she'd stumble. We finally managed it by having Monica arch her back up first, then squat, and then pull herself upright, using the snowmobile for balance. She grabbed my legs and hiked me up around her hips.

"There. Just like the pony rides I used to give you when we were little. Do you remember?" Monica asked.

"Not really," I said. "Tell me."

As Monica and I headed back to the retreat center, she told me about our younger days when I was just a kid in diapers. When the memories got to a point that I could relate, I added my version of things.

"Those were fun days, weren't they?" I said.

"Yeah, they were."

We were silent for a while, hearing only the steady, heavy rhythm of Monica's breathing and the jingling of EJ's collar beside us.

"I miss those days, Monica," I said, leaning my head against her hair. My heart added one more feeling. "And I miss you."

"Me too," she said. "I'm sorry, Darcy. I'm sorry for what I said. And not just the other day at the chalet with the guys. I'm sorry about that awful evening by the dishwasher. You're not self-centered. At least not any more than Josh or me."

"Really? You mean you don't think my wheelchair is always the center of things?"

Monica hiked me up higher on her back. "So what if it is? That's just a fact of life, right? Besides, you're worth it. You're my sister!"

A flood of peace all mixed up with joy washed through me. At the same time, I fought back tears. "Sometimes I feel so . . . so irked that my wheelchair forces everybody in the family to change their plans. You know . . . how all of us have to take it into consideration before we do anything."

We were quiet as we trudged on further, as if we both knew we were getting to the bottom of it all. It was an honest moment, and neither of us wanted to break the spell.

After a few minutes Monica added, "Darcy, you've been through a lot. It's me who's been self-centered, spending so much time with Doug. If it hadn't been for me, you wouldn't have gotten upset and taken off on the snowmobile and. . . ."

I couldn't see her face, but I could tell she was

starting to cry.

"That's okay, Monica," I interrupted. "There's lots of things neither of us should have said or even thought. But that's all behind us. Let's just get home and be sisters again."

The hike back was very hard on her. We stopped to rest every once in a while by leaning back against a tree, my body pinned between hers and the trunk. It wasn't much help, but it was better than nothing. EJ served as our encourager, running on ahead every once in a while, barking and wagging his tail.

It took us over an hour to get back, but we talked about a lot of things and a lot of feelings. The pine trees gave us protection from the wind, and the sun peeked out from the clouds and kept us warm.

My heart didn't need the sun. Being close to Monica gave me all the warmth I needed. *We're sisters again*, I repeated to myself over and over.

By the time we got back to the retreat center, a search party had been organized. We heard snowmobiles being revved up in the distance and saw the flashing lights of an emergency truck through the trees. Shouts of "Darcy!" and "Monica!" were everywhere.

"Over here, Dad!" Monica yelled as we got within sight of the snowmobile shed. Dad and Mom, as well as Chip and Mandy, pushed their way through a group of people who had gathered in the parking lot. Chip grabbed EJ as he bounded toward them.

"Where in the world have you been?" Dad asked

as he lifted me off of Monica's back. As Monica dropped to her knees, a couple of men from the emergency truck put a blanket over her and poured her something hot from a thermos.

The emergency guys sat me on the front seat of the truck and checked us over. Except for ice cold fingers and toes and a warning that I should get my leg x-rayed, we were fine.

The crowd thinned out, and Dad lifted me into his arms to take me back to the cabin.

"We thought you'd decided to take up skiing!!" he said, trying to make light of what could have been a real disaster. He nodded toward Chip, who still had EJ in tow. "Chip, would you go tell the others in the dining hall that we found them?"

"Sure, Mr. DeAngelis," Chip answered. He smiled at me. "I'm glad you're safe, Darcy. I was worried about you. I'm sorry I didn't stay with you before."

"Don't think about it," I said as I looked over my dad's shoulder. "I wouldn't have let you anyway. You know how stubborn I can be. And I'm sorry I got upset at you. You were right, you know."

I didn't want to tell Chip what he was right about in front of my dad and mom. But judging from the soft look in his eyes, he knew what I meant. I had been jealous of Monica and Doug and their boyfriend-girlfriend thing. But looking at Chip—who I decided right then and there should be elevated to best-friend status—I realized that the boyfriend stuff didn't matter. He was my friend, my special friend. And he knew it.

Chip gave a thumbs-up sign, yelled, "C'mon, EJ," and took off to deliver the message to the rest of the people from our church.

Dad was huffing by the time we reached the front door of our cabin.

"I've got the bed ready," Mom said. "Let's change her clothes."

We entered the bedroom, and Dad laid me down on the bed.

"Something hot to drink?" Monica asked.

"Sounds good," I said, my teeth chattering.

"One hot chocolate coming up! I'll get it from the dining hall. And a chocolate chip cookie for dunking too," she said with a smile. She was remembering the kindness I had tried to show her on the ski slopes. "I'll be right back with the most awesome chocolate rescue platter you've ever seen. Wanna help, Mandy?"

Mandy nodded. She hadn't spoken a word since my return, but there were tears in her eyes. She hugged me tightly as I lay on the bed. "I'm so glad you're back."

"Monica," I called out as Mandy left to catch up with her.

She yelled back, "What?" from the front steps.

"Thanks for being my sister."

"Same here," she said, and the two of them left.

Mom took off my boots and peeled off my wet jeans. She pulled some dry things from the suitcase and changed me into warm clothes. I could hear Chip and EJ coming back up the path. Josh was with them too.

"Boy, EJ, you ought to get an award," I heard Josh say. "You're a real lifesaver dog!" They all came through the front door.

"So how did EJ find me, anyway?" I asked my dad.

"Beats me, Darcy," he said. "But I do know how he got out of the yard. Seems he learned how to push his paw down on the latch. I guess that's the way he's been getting out all weekend. He just opened the gate by himself!"

"You mean like the dogs at Canine Companions?" I asked.

"Seems so. Maybe he picked up the idea from reading one of your brochures!"

I looked over at EJ, who was wrestling with Josh.

"Come here, EJ," I said. "Come here, boy."

He obeyed me instantly and came to sit next to my bed. He laid his head near my pillow, his nose just inches away from my mine. He had been happy and panting, but now he just closed his mouth and looked at me.

"Thank you, EJ. You saved my life. Maybe you didn't know what you were doing, but Dr. T was right. All that really counts is having a dog that really loves you."

EJ's dark brown eyes were as gentle as they had always been, even when I had scolded him. He had never given up on me. He was a true friend.

"You are now my official service dog, EJ," I said as I hugged his neck.

EJ shook his head and barked, Golden

Retrieverese for "I knew that all along."

Mom, Dad, Chip, and Josh all applauded our new hero.

And thank You, too, Lord. You've taught me that if I've "got it," then "thank it." And right now, I've got more then I could ever thank You for. You're the best!

Darcy

"Let's have a Feel-Sorry-for-Darcy Day."

That's what Darcy's sister says when Darcy sulks over having to stay with her parents at family camp, instead of rooming with the other girls her age. Once more, her wheelchair has set her apart.

Darcy is tired of being different. Tired of putting up a good front. Tired of putting up with insensitive remarks. Tired of being left out. But her time at camp brings some surprises, and Darcy learns more than she could have imagined about prayer, about God, about her friends . . . and about herself.

JONI EARECKSON TADA has been in a wheelchair herself since she was seventeen. Her story has been told in the books *Joni* and *Choices/Changes* and the film *Joni*. The Christian Fund for the Disabled, an organization that Joni started, works to bring together disabled people and caring churches.

Chariot Books
David C. Cook Publishing Co.

Darcy and the Meanest Teacher in the World

**"Don't be silly, Darcy.
I suggest you find more suitable activities."**

Mrs. Crowhurst's abrupt putdown in front of a gymfull of seventh graders leaves Darcy angry and humiliated. It isn't that Darcy cares so deeply about being manager of the girls' basketball team—it's just that "The Crow" seems to have it in for her.

Darcy decides to do some investigative journalism for the school paper on the topic of mean teachers. She's sure that her "expose" will win her the respect and admiration of her peers—not to mention their votes when she runs for president of the student government.

But why aren't her faithful sidekicks, Mandy and Chip, very enthusiastic about her project? And why doesn't she want her parents or journalism advisor to know what she's up to?

JONI EARECKSON TADA has been in a wheelchair herself since she was seventeen. Her story has been told in the books *Joni* and *Choices/Changes* and the film *Joni*.

Chariot Books
David C. Cook Publishing Co.

Meet My Friends

Three stories of ordinary kids ... with EXTRAordinary courage.

Have you ever wondered what life would be like if you couldn't see? or hear? or walk? Aimee, Jamie, and Josh can tell you.

Except for their disabilities, they're pretty ordinary kids. They enjoy sports, talk to God, have pets, fight with little brothers, and want to be liked by their classmates at school. In fact, they're a lot like you.

Their stories are told by JONI EARECKSON TADA, who's been in a wheelchair herself since she was seventeen. Since then, God has taken Joni on some great adventures. She's met a lot of grown-ups and kids with different kinds of disabilities. And she's found that behind the handicaps are real, ordinary people with real, ordinary hopes and fears and dreams ... and a lot of courage.

Come along with Joni ... and meet her friends!

Chariot Books
David C. Cook Publishing Co.